C000055889

Sherlock Holmes and the Lyme Regis Horror

– DAVID RUFFLE–

FASTPRINT PUBLISHING
PETERBOROUGH, ENGLAND

SHERLOCK HOLMES AND THE LYME REGIS HORROR
Copyright © David Ruffle 2009

All rights reserved.

No part of this book may be reproduced in any form by
photocopying or any electronic or mechanical means,
including information storage or retrieval systems,
without permission in writing from both the copyright
owner and the publisher of the book.

ISBN 978-184426-722-4

First published 2009 by
FASTPRINT PUBLISHING
Peterborough, England.

Printed with kind permission of Jonathan Clowes Ltd,
London, on behalf of Andrea Plunket, the Administrator of the Sir Arthur
Conan Doyle Copyrights.

Printed by
www.printondemand-worldwide.com

Dedicated to Gill Stammers.
To me, she will always be *the* woman.

EDITOR'S NOTE

Shortly after moving to Lyme Regis in the summer of 2004 I came across an oral tradition that Sherlock Holmes and Dr. Watson had once visited the town. The same may be true of many towns throughout the country which seek to lay claim to a celebrated and justly famous pair, I do not know. This oral tradition outlines how the good doctor had been, in fact, a frequent visitor to Lyme.

Being a life long Holmes aficionado, I decided I had to find out more. As you can imagine, I pored over history books, Victorian journals, in fact anything which I thought might furnish me with documentary evidence for such a tale. My efforts were met with a spectacular lack of success. Old bundles of yellowing newspapers were examined in minute detail in the manner of Holmes himself. If there was written evidence of such visits, then it was surely lost or the stories of the visits themselves were apocryphal. I settled myself just to enjoy the legend as an added bonus to the delights of living here.

Some time later, I moved house and found myself temporarily in the 'old town' in Coombe Street. After a day or two of frenzied unpacking, I had whole rooms full of empty boxes, these I removed to the loft, just throwing them in, in any old fashion.

Habitually a tidy person, my conscience got the better of me and back I went to the loft to tidy up my mess. There was the usual debris present of past owners. I sifted through some of these and consigned much of it to various bin bags. I then saw what appeared to be an ill fitting smallish wall panel, looking as though a previous tenant or owner had carried out a hurried repair. I pulled on it to test its strength and the whole thing gave way. Neatly tucked away inside was a sheaf of papers tied with a ribbon. I pulled the ribbon away and the first thing I really noticed were the words 'John H. Watson.' The tidying could now wait. I took my treasure downstairs and could not believe my eyes when I realised what in fact it was, an adventure purporting to come from the pen of Watson himself.

I devoured the contents in one sitting, but could I be sure it was genuine? I sent the manuscript to have it compared with the few known examples of Watson's handwriting; the reports I received back were favourable without being totally conclusive. The paper and ink seemed to belong to the Victorian era, but again I can offer no proof as to its authenticity. However, I am entirely confident that this account was written by Watson on one of his subsequent visits to Lyme and it is a true account of what Holmes and the good doctor faced on their initial visit here. I have taken it upon myself to correct one or two errors regarding Lyme's history in the spirit of accuracy. The manuscript was quite faded here and there and again I have taken it upon myself to add the odd word or sentence, which I feel approximate to the missing ones, other than that the tale is presented here, just as Watson wrote it down, over one hundred years ago.

Along with this newly discovered tale, I have included a few short offerings of mine; all involve Holmes and Watson and/or Lyme Regis, in some of which, I have tried my hand at writing in a Watsonian style.

David Ruffle Lyme Regis 2009.

CHAPTER ONE

I *pick up my pen to write this account in the full knowledge it may never see the light of day. It was an adventure which will chill me to the bone to my dying day and one which the public would find scarcely credible. However, I feel I owe it to myself for personal reasons and to Holmes, to set down a record of it, for, in all our time together, never had we faced such an evil, unimaginable horror as that which we encountered on the quiet Dorsetshire coast.*

John H. Watson, Lyme Regis 1897.

It was a Friday in late May 1896. The day had dawned bright after heavy overnight rain which had woken me on more than one occasion. I bestirred myself and dressed for any inclement weather I may encounter and headed somewhat optimistically for that bastion of all that is good in England, Lords Cricket Ground.

Play commenced late due to the effect of the rain on the pitch, but it was still a stirring example of the cut and thrust of county cricket. A match destined for a draw was brought to a result by the vagaries of the English weather and fine play. Middlesex's opponents were the redoubtable Yorkshire and although the latter were behind on the first innings, the combination of a drying pitch and the artistry of Bobby Peel's bowling did for Middlesex and Tunnicliffe with his opening partner Brown hit off the one hundred and forty seven runs needed to win as the sun beat down.

All of which I was doing my best to relate to Holmes who was languishing with his thin, long form curled up, almost feline like, in the recesses of his armchair. My best efforts to engage my friend's attention and interest were met with a singular lack of success and the only outward signs he had indeed heard a word I had uttered were the occasional grunts which emanated from his direction. With a sudden lithe movement he sprang to his feet and interrupted my flow. "My dear fellow, your attempts to regale me with tales of sporting prowess are most entertaining, but of little or no interest to me, alas."

"But, Holmes," I remonstrated, "I am describing to you a sweet and healthy world."

He put a long thin hand up. "Yes, Watson I am sure you are right in what you say, but insofar as the sporting world does not impinge upon my professional activities, then it must remain a subject in which I cannot share your evident enthusiasm."

Determined not to be browbeaten by my friend, I gamely soldiered on, "But surely, Holmes, cricket stands for all that we love in this country; honour and an inherent sense of duty and fair play."

"Tsk, Watson, show me fifty cricketers and I will show you at least ten who disregard that fine code you mention and cheat, subtle though their ways may be."

Holmes had remarked before that I had a grand gift of silence. I now exercised that gift and settled down to read the newspaper, knowing as always, that no good would come of pursuing an argument with my companion.

As Holmes resumed his languishing and silence, I glanced through the 'Times' noticing how he had ringed several items in the agony columns to which he always turned to eagerly. On many occasions the whole tide of cases he had been working on had turned because of what he had read and deduced from the guarded and to me, frankly mystifying messages in its columns. Nothing today had seemingly sparked his interest or exercised his immense intellect. Without a case to utilise his talents he was prone to lying around motionless and inert with barely a word passing his lips. At times like this I was concerned for his well-being as both his friend and physician. I could not help, but glance to the leather bound morocco case there on the mantelpiece and would fervently pray that my friend's ennui would not drive him once more to that seven percent solution which he found so stimulating.

My reverie was broken into by Holmes, "If you care to look on the luncheon tray you will find a letter there for you."

I was not overly surprised the letter should have found itself on the tray amongst the remains of Holmes's luncheon, indeed I was only too pleased that my unopened correspondence had not ended up like Holmes's own, affixed to the wooden mantelpiece by a jack-knife.

A little while later my thoughts were once more interrupted by my friend, "I rather think, Watson that a trip to Lyme Regis to see an old friend from your university days would be a capital idea."

"In the name of all that's sacred, Holmes," I cried, "have you read the contents of a private letter in order to pull off this mind-reading trick?"

"Really, Watson, I would hope you know me better than that. No, my deduction, which has obviously hit the mark, was based on observation pure and simple."

"I cannot see what I could have possibly done to enable you to make such a deduction," I replied.

"My dear fellow, you always remain perplexed at these little parlour games of mine and yet when I explain my reasoning as revealed to me by your features and movements, you will no doubt declare it to be most elementary."

"Nevertheless, Holmes, I would be grateful if you could reveal to me the workings of that fine intellect and tell me how you arrived at that conclusion." My friend was entirely susceptible to flattery and my well chosen words brought forth his explanation with an undeniable flush of pleasure.

"Very well, Watson, after reading through the contents of the letter you sat back and smiled with the countenance of one recalling their youth. You then glanced up at your framed diploma from the University of London, thereby alerting me to the fact that this was almost certainly a missive from a friend of those far off days. Your next action was to then walk to the bookcase, where you opened up a copy of Jane Austen's overly romantic novel 'Persuasion', to a page which I believe equates to an episode where one of her chief characters foolishly jumps down some steps on the buttress known as The Cobb in the seaside town of Lyme Regis. As you returned to your seat your hand briefly lighted upon the Bradshaw's, at which point I interrupted your thoughts to your obvious consternation and surprise."

"Most elementary, Holmes," I said on cue.

"I am glad you agree my friend," he said, smiling, "I would be a dullard indeed if I could not interpret that evidence."

"Have you decided whether to take up your old friend's kind invitation?" Holmes continued.

"I think I shall, Holmes, the letter is from my old friend Godfrey Jacobs, of whom I have the happiest memories from our joint studies, not to mention of course, our occasional rugby matches together for Blackheath under the captaincy of Stokes." I saw my friend wince at yet another mention of sport so I moved on quickly, "he is now in practice in Lyme Regis as you correctly *guessed*," I said, slightly mockingly, as I knew my friend would take umbrage at my use of the word.

"Tch, tch, Watson, you of all people should know I never guess," Holmes snapped back, yet smiling all the while.

"Yes, I know full well that guessing is destructive to the logical faculties, but if I were to guess or rather deduce, I would say that you have no case in hand at the moment."

"Excellent my dear fellow, we shall make a detective out of you yet," Holmes answered cheerily. "No, Watson, as you deduced so correctly, I have no case in hand at the moment, no perplexing problem to probe, hence the listless being you see before you. The truth is my dear fellow that I am stagnating day by day. The crimes that do come my way are so exceedingly commonplace that even the most dull-witted of the Scotland Yarders would solve them easily."

"Well, Holmes....." I began.

"The question you are about to propose is most transparent, Doctor and the answer I fear, must be no."

I knew of course, my friend would see where my mind was going, but I was not one for giving up. "But, Holmes, just think, a well deserved break, fresh sea air in one of our loveliest counties, just what the doctor ordered or, at any rate, this particular doctor."

"I appreciate your concern *Doctor*," he said stressing the last word, "but you know full well how my absence from the capital excites members of the criminal classes. I fear your trip to Lyme Regis will have to take place without me."

"But, Holmes," I protested, "you yourself said that crime is commonplace these days; there are no Moriartys or Morans to engage you in a battle of wits."

"That much is certainly true, but what would you have me do, sit and gaze upon the sea like a retired Major, devoid of all purpose in his life? I need work. I need problems for this engine of mine to operate efficiently."

I tried another approach; one which I thought may well bear fruit. "I have heard you speak of William Buckland, latterly Dean of Westminster and how much you admired his speculative intelligence and non-conformity."

"Yes indeed, Watson, I believe he was a man from whom we can all learn and as a scientist, was, I believe unique, although, sadly, that did not prevent him from declining into madness in his later years."

"Among the points in the letter you did not guess, I am sorry Holmes, I mean *deduce*." I corrected myself, smiling, "was the information that there is to be an exhibition of this fellow's work throughout June in Lyme Regis."

"Hah! A distinct touch, Watson," Holmes laughed in that peculiar silent fashion of his, "you have cast your bait like bread upon the water and you have succeeded in reeling me in. Very well, Lyme Regis it is, my friend."

Although Holmes had no cases to occupy him at that time, there were still ramifications to be dealt with from his last investigation, which had resulted in the round up of the notorious Charles gang of Middleton Cheney in one of our northern shires. It was a masterpiece of deduction by my friend, indeed to my mind, it was one of his finest moments. His brilliance in this case was a marvel to behold and one day the full story may be told when some of the principals in the case can no longer be harmed by certain revelations that must unavoidably come out. Until that time it must remain in my dispatch box with many other such cases.

In the days before we set off on what I termed a holiday and what Holmes no doubt saw in other terms, I had further correspondence with Jacobs. He was now possessed of a young family and as his cottage was, but a small one, he had arranged accommodation for us at a local boarding house under very favourable rates. This establishment was run by a Mrs. Heidler and Jacobs assured us that we would be very well looked after should we wish to avail ourselves of those terms. I wired that they would be perfectly acceptable and we looked forward to meeting Mrs. Heidler, also to seeing Jacobs and his family.

On the appointed day we said our farewells to Mrs. Hudson and set off in a Hansom cab to that great terminus Waterloo.

CHAPTER TWO

The station was a hubbub of noise and activity and I could not help, but be reminded of my return to the metropolis after being invalided out of the Army. On that previous occasion I had arrived here after a lengthy railway journey from Portsmouth, full of hope and optimism in picking up my life again in spite of my health being ruined irretrievably due to injuries received during the Battle of Maiwand. As I took in the sights, sounds and smells I found my hand stealing involuntarily towards my old wound, where sixteen years before a Jezail bullet had shattered the bone and grazed the subclavian artery. How my life had changed since those days and in ways I could not have possibly foreseen.

It was a fine morning and Holmes was busying himself purchasing newspapers for the journey. I could see his tall, gaunt figure, looking even taller and gaunter in his Inverness cape and ear-flapped travelling cap. We found a carriage to ourselves and Holmes immediately applied himself to a diligent and thorough perusal of the morning newspapers. When each one had been completed, he would roll it into a ball; stuff it behind the cushion, under the seat or even upon the luggage rack despite my reproachful glances at him. It was the loveliest of spring days, the sun was bright overhead and even Holmes appeared to be entranced by what he saw as we rolled through the countryside. Yet, I knew he saw, not the beauty I did, looking instead beyond the superficial attractiveness of the scattered rural dwellings; observing them from his own particular viewpoint and seeing the impunity with which crimes may be committed there. It was his belief, as he stated to me once, that the lowest and vilest alleys in London do not present a more dreadful record of sin than does the smiling and beautiful countryside.

My own reading material was slight; in addition to the yellow-backed novel I had brought along, I also had a gazetteer and a brief history of Lyme Regis and its environs, which I was reading avidly.

"I think, Holmes," I ventured, "that we will find much to occupy ourselves in the town. It has a fascinating history including being besieged by the Royalist forces in the Civil War and of course the Duke of Monmouth's fateful rebellion had its starting point in Lyme in 1685."

"I, for my part will confine myself to the exhibition of Professor Buckland's work and also a study of the local geology which I am given to understand is quite singular," Holmes replied. "The Dorsetshire dialect also presents many points of interest to me and has much in common with the rhythms of the trading language used by the early Phoenicians. Indeed, I hope to be able to establish an historical link between Lyme Regis and that distant land."

"Has there been research into this field previously, Holmes?" I inquired.

"A little, yes, but I am hopeful of producing the definitive work on the subject. As you know, language and its usage is by way of being a hobby of mine and I have published a small monograph on ancient English dialects which I commend to you, it is reckoned to be the final word on the subject."

"Holmes, I cannot see how you possibly have the time to embark on such a project, surely you are already punishing your body and brain far too much."

"I assure you my dear fellow, I would punish them even more through inactivity; my constitution is most peculiar in that I am never tired through work, be it mental or physical, but idleness, ah, Doctor, that will drain me completely."

"We all need to rest sometimes, even you," I said pointedly.

I resumed my reading and Holmes lit his pipe. All too soon the carriage resembled our sitting room at Baker Street in miniature, with clouds of acrid smoke permeating into all the nooks and crannies. Holmes seemed to have a special gift of turning wherever he was into a home from home, as was the case here, with papers strewn carelessly around and outer clothes in an untidy heap where they had fallen after being discarded.

As the train rumbled on, the seasonal warmth of the sun shining through the window and the gentle motion of the wheels on the tracks soon had me in the arms of Morpheus. I was awakened by Holmes who informed me that we would shortly be arriving in Axminster. I gathered both my thoughts and belongings and said to Holmes as I looked out of the carriage window, "You are right Holmes, for I observe we are now travelling at the rate of twenty five miles per hour only."

Holmes glanced at me quizzically.

"The telegraph poles are sixty-five yards apart, Holmes, it is, but a simple calculation you know."

Holmes gave me a withering look, "Upon my word, Watson, you never fail to amaze me old fellow."

David Ruffle

CHAPTER THREE

Jacobs had arranged the provision of a dog-cart to meet us and bring us the six miles down into Lyme Regis, but we could see no sign of it as we waited outside Axminster station. There were one or two families also awaiting some form of transport. The children looked most excited to be this close to the sea and who could fail to be moved by the joy on their faces, their tiny hands clutching buckets and spades? I motioned Holmes to observe the scene and he did so with barely a smile on his face, his machine-like countenance seemingly unmoved by the rapture that was provoked in me by these children and their sheer happiness. I had never lost my love for the sea and I remembered with great pleasure the holidays I had spent with my father and mother, together with my brother Henry at Southsea. Thinking of my poor brother, I patted my inside pocket which contained a handsome watch. It had once belonged to my father and had been handed down to my brother and thence to me after his untimely and sad death.

Holmes noted my movements and gave me a gentle smile which spoke volumes for his humanity, at times like these I would be willing to swear he had the ability to read my innermost thoughts. Indeed, on many an occasion, he did precisely that to my mind.

"I was just reminiscing, Holmes, revisiting my childhood," I said, by way of explanation.

Holmes looked at me and nodding sagely, remarked, "I understand and I envy you the happy memories you possess in abundance, even when those self same memories have the ability to cause you sadness and pain too."

It was not long after my brother's death that sweet Mary Morstan came into my life. She shared my burden of sadness and the feelings of irrational guilt that I should be living while my brother lay in his grave and now she was gone too, taken from me so cruelly three short years ago. It was a time when I was truly alone, believing like the rest of the world that Holmes himself was dead, having fought his bitter duel with Moriarty to the end and beyond, culminating in the deaths of the most dangerous criminal and the foremost champion of the law of their generation in the swirling waters below the Reichenbach Falls. Then, Holmes, to my complete amazement and utter joy, came back from the 'dead' and my shattered life began to be rebuilt slowly, but surely. Holmes remained the one constant in my life, my one loyal and trusted friend.

A gnarled old man alighted from a dog cart and approached us. He was bewhiskered and lugubrious looking with a somewhat hesitant manner, "Er....would you be the gentlemen from London for Master Jacobs?" he asked slowly. When Holmes replied in the affirmative he proffered his own name, "I be William Curtis, Master Jacobs has sent me to collect you gentlemen."

"Capital," said Holmes. "Very well, Curtis, we are more than ready, let's be off." With that we threw our luggage into the back of the cart, clambered in ourselves and set off for Lyme Regis. The ride took us through Axminster with its fine old church dominating the centre of that lovely, ancient town. Within minutes however, we were in open countryside, trotting through leafy lanes which gave way to rolling fields and the dotted cottages of a hamlet or two. Curtis was greeted pleasantly by a few people we passed and indeed, there seemed an agreeable air of friendliness emanating from the whole of this area. As we passed through the village of Uplyme I was more than pleased to see that most English of sports taking place, a game of cricket, played merely for the love of the game with no thought of reward. I stole a gleeful glance at my friend who merely sighed and rolled his eyes and I thought better of enthusing on the scene. Barely one mile further on, we arrived in Lyme Regis and at once began a descent which afforded us a wondrous view of the sea beyond the houses and cottages.

Curtis addressed us for the first time since leaving Axminster, "Master Jacobs has asked me to convey you gentlemen directly to Mrs. Heidler's, as he be with his patients for a time yet."

"Thank you Curtis, that will be admirable," I said.

We turned to the left and descended another hill leading to an exceedingly narrow street that Curtis identified for us as Coombe Street.

We passed over a small, cramped bridge, with a river trickling and gurgling away beneath it and within yards Curtis pulled up outside a cream-coloured three storey house.

"This be Mrs. Heidler's then gentlemen," Curtis said, "her be expecting you."

We dropped to our feet and retrieved our luggage as Curtis drove off. I knocked on the door and it was opened by a sallow looking youth who said not a word, but merely stared at us in a sullen manner.

"My name is Dr. Watson and this is my friend Mr. Sherlock Holmes, we are given to understand that Mrs. Heidler is expecting us, will you please inform her that we have arrived?"

In response, he opened the door wider and with a sweep of his arm motioned for us to enter. We followed him down a long passageway and from there into a small, but homely parlour. There, seated at a table was the lady of the house. She rose and came over to us. "Welcome to Lyme Regis, Mr. Holmes and Dr. Watson, my name is Mrs. Heidler." As she said this she had come into the light given off by an adjacent gas lamp and for a brief moment I thought I was going to faint for only the second time in my life. With her blonde hair, large blue eyes and such a sweet, amiable expression, she was the very image of my own beautiful Mary. Holmes must have noticed my discomfiture for he placed a hand on my elbow as if to steady me.

"Thank you, Mrs.Heidler for your most warm welcome," Holmes said and then to me in a hushed aside, "are you all right,

Watson? I have to admit, I too was struck by the resemblance to the good Mrs.Watson."

"Yes, quite all right now, Holmes and thank you." I too offered my greetings to Mrs. Heidler and hoped that my momentary bewilderment had not become apparent to her.

CHAPTER FOUR

"You must be tired after such a long journey, let me show you to your rooms gentlemen, so that you may freshen up," Mrs.Heidler offered.

"Thank you, Mrs. Heidler that will be most welcome," Holmes said.

We collected our belongings and followed her up some rickety stairs to the top floor where we were shown two very well appointed rooms which would certainly fulfil our needs over the next few days. Mrs. Heidler informed us that she would be preparing a late luncheon if we wished to partake. I, for one was glad to hear it, my food intake was rather more regular than Holmes's own. Mealtimes had come and gone many times without so much as a morsel passing our lips whilst in the midst of one of our adventures. Although my constitution demanded food as soon as was humanly possible, Holmes, much to my chagrin would go for days without so much as a crumb, his thin, eager features becoming even more pronounced as he lost himself in a particularly difficult, abstruse problem.

We hurried through the process of unpacking and returned downstairs to the small parlour. There was a most delightful luncheon laid out which we set about doing justice to. It was honest, simple fare, but none the less palatable for that. During the repast Mrs. Heidler volunteered an account as to how she had ended up in this most delightful spot. The sallow youth who had opened the door to us was formally introduced as Mrs. Heidler's son, Nathaniel who was coming up to sixteen years old and when not assisting his mother in the running of this establishment, worked as a boot boy at The Royal Lion in Broad Street. Mrs. Heidler had been widowed when her husband Henry had died as a result of wounds suffered at the Battle of Majuba Hill during the Boer War. Through no fault of her own she found herself in somewhat impoverished circumstances with an eight month old son to care for. Whilst many women of the tender age of twenty two have much to look forward to, Mrs. Heidler had no great reason to be optimistic regarding her future. Fortuitously, salvation arrived through a maiden aunt in Lyme Regis, who being of advanced years needed someone to help with the everyday chores in return for board and lodging. The arrangement turned out to be admirable to both parties and continued until the death of the aunt some five years ago, when the house then became Mrs. Heidler's under the terms of the Will and Last Testament of her Aunt Letitia. Since that date Mrs Heidler had cleared the rooms in the house that had formerly been her aunt's private rooms and had proceeded to take in paying guests, which provided her with a modest living.

"I fear I must apologise gentlemen, for rambling on so," she said.

"Not at all, Mrs. Heidler," I said. "It was a most interesting account; you have done very well for yourself since those dark days."

"Thank you, Dr. Watson, you are most kind," Mrs. Heidler said, smiling a very warm smile.

As she smiled at me, I travelled back in my mind to a warm July day in 1888 when Mary Morstan had been ushered into the presence of Holmes and I. She brought with her a fascinating case involving murder, revenge and precious pearls, but there was no pearl more precious on God's earth to me than that sweet smile of hers as she raised a gloved hand and asked me to stay with Holmes and listen to her tale. Before that initial interview had come to a close I had lost my heart completely to Miss Morstan. How the woman seated opposite me reminded me of her and what tortures it was already beginning to give me.

The voice of my dear friend returned reason to me. "Watson, have you arranged a time for us to visit your friend, Dr. Jacobs?"

"Not a firm time, I intimated we would arrive maybe a few minutes after five o' clock when his surgery closes," I replied.

"Very well my dear fellow, why not take advantage of this fine Spring weather, and allow ourselves a constitutional, the better to explore this place?"

"A capital notion, Holmes," I adjoined.

We thanked Mrs. Heidler profusely for the splendid luncheon, donned our coats and set out to stroll around this beautiful town. By walking east and then seaward along the length of Coombe Street we soon arrived at what was named 'The Square'. There stood the Lyme Regis Assembly Rooms, modelled it is said, upon those of Bath, but sadly, due to its cramped location, appearing neither as grand nor as imposing as that of its progenitor. I noted with interest that there was a Grand Dance to take place on the morrow and declared to Holmes that I may well have a mind to attend. He, in the meantime had been looking at the Victoria Hall which was to be found to the side of the Assembly Rooms. It was there that the exhibition of William Buckland's work was displayed and I deduced that Holmes would find that of greater interest than a mere dance. His work, the exercise of his intellect was where Holmes found his enjoyment, not for him the bagatelles of dances and balls. Admittedly, he did derive pleasure from the occasional concerts he attended, but even then I thought it was more the science of music that appealed to his orderly mind rather than the pleasure of the music itself. Indeed, his own compositions on the violin seemed to me to be more scientific than rhythmic or melodious, but it was not a theory which I expounded to Holmes!

We walked on in companionable silence, gazing out to sea as we did so. It was a most exquisite sight. The brilliant sunshine coupled with the deep blue sky rendered the surface of the sea a lovely cerulean colour. There were a few bathing machines in use and children splashing happily as they paddled in the sea. Seagulls wheeled overhead and called to their neighbours. This part of Lyme was aptly named 'The Walk' and took us the length of the sea front until we reached the Cobb, a huge and ancient breakwater which had been protecting the town from the worst of storms for over five hundred years and also creating a safe, natural harbour. The whole vista from this viewpoint was a veritable feast for the eyes. It had been a long time since I had come across a scene quite as beautiful as this.

"Do you know, Holmes, that when Alfred, Lord Tennyson made his first ever visit to Lyme, his initial request before he could be enticed to see anything else was to be shown the very spot where Louisa Musgrove had fallen on the Cobb in 'Persuasion' ?"

"Indeed, Watson? I must confess I was not aware of it, but neither am I greatly surprised by it, the poetic mind does seem to run contrary to normal human values," he replied.

"Pshaw, Holmes, I am more and more convinced there is no romance in that soul of yours."

"What need have I of romance?" he said, almost to himself and a little sadly I thought too.

There was a hurry-scurry of activity in the harbour, coal was being offloaded from a ship to the quayside, also timber being brought ashore from what appeared to be a Russian ship, if I had managed to translate the markings accurately. It was the kind of activity which would have gone on here for many hundreds of years, if Holmes was correct in his theory of Phoenician traders disembarking here to sell their wares. From the Cobb we had a fine view of the eastern seaboard and thence to the cliffs which stretched away towards Weymouth, it was well nigh perfect to my eyes. We strolled back the way we had come, pausing only to take in more sights and sounds. Even Holmes seemed to be impressed by what he was seeing; his senses appeared to be heightened as opposed to the lethargy that I usually witnessed when he found himself without a case.

"Are you enjoying yourself, Holmes?" I asked.

"Yes my dear fellow, much to your surprise I have no doubt. I am particularly intrigued by the local speech patterns that I am picking up as we pass people by; it bodes well for my investigations into their source."

"Holmes, can you not just have a simple holiday for once?" I admonished.

"For me, Watson, this is precisely that, but under my own terms. I cannot allow my mind to stagnate, work is essential to my well being as I have expressed to you on many occasions."

I had to agree with him. I had seen firsthand what lethargy and ennui did to Holmes and I had no wish to re-visit those depths of despair with him.

Upon reaching the Assembly Rooms once more, we turned left and walked up the main street which is adorned with the name Broad Street. The name seemed a misnomer to me, but then again, compared with the only street we had so far encountered perhaps it wasn't so fanciful after all. Broad Street was well stocked with shops and suppliers, at least two tailors, a chemist, a tobacconist who was also the local hairdresser, a watchmaker and jeweller and a tea shop amongst others. We also came across The Royal Lion where Nathaniel worked as a boot boy and another hostelry too, The Three Cups. It was a busy, bustling street. By now we had reached the top of Broad Street which afforded us wonderful views back down to the sea. Holmes was preoccupied, intent on listening to the dialect being spoken, so I drank in the scene alone and in peace!

The greater part of the afternoon had passed most agreeably and now we found ourselves at the top of Sherborne Lane, an ancient trackway, narrow, confined and exceedingly steep, but fortunately on this occasion we would be descending rather than ascending. Jacobs lived in Chapel Cottage, which he assured us we would find very easily and in this he was proved correct. Jacobs answered the door immediately upon my knock and grabbed me firmly by the hand, grinning from ear to ear.

"It is so good to see you again, Watson," he enthused. "It has been far too long my old friend."

We had kept in touch via regular letters, but these fell away to almost nothing after a few years as can often happen to the greatest of friendships.

"And you too, it must be all of fifteen years since we last saw each other," said I.

"Yes, if I remember correctly, you had just arrived back from Afghanistan and were looking for rooms or something of the sort."

"Yes and then purely by chance, thanks to a meeting with Stamford, whom I am sure you remember well, I met up with Holmes in Barts just two days later and we set up in our Baker Street rooms together."

"I am sorry, my dear fellow," I said, looking at Holmes, "let me introduce you, Jacobs, this is my very good friend, Mr. Sherlock Holmes."

"A very great pleasure to meet you Mr. Holmes, I am Dr. Godfrey Jacobs as you must have worked out, both of you please come in and meet my family, my boys in particular love your adventures that Watson details so faithfully and they have been looking forward with great excitement to meeting you."

"Do you not find the life down here a little quiet, Jacobs?" I asked.

"Mostly, yes, if I am perfectly honest," he laughed. "Although just recently there have been some most curious events which have livened things up somewhat."

At the mention of 'curious events' Holmes looked at Jacobs in a most intense manner.

"Watson here will tell you, I can never resist the curious, it often has a habit of leading on to much deeper things and besides I am a student of all that falls outside of the normal. May we expect an account of these events later, Doctor?" Holmes asked.

CHAPTER FIVE

"I promise you a full account later, Mr. Holmes, although I fear you are liable to be disappointed, but first, my family awaits," Jacobs replied as we stepped over the threshold.

He ushered us into the sitting-room and there as promised, we met his family. His wife, Sarah rose to greet us. She was tall and graceful with long, flowing dark hair. In attendance on each side of her, were two delightful children who seemed to be in awe of us.

"A pleasure to meet you both, Dr. Watson and Mr. Holmes," she said. "Please allow me to introduce our two lovely boys, Arthur and Cecil. Say hullo to our visitors please, boys."

By way of response we got stares and a mumbled greeting.

"Hullo, boys," I said, kneeling down to their level. "Now, I wonder who is the eldest.....?"

"Me." said the tallest one. "I'm Arthur. I'm nine years old."

"And how old are you Cecil?" I asked.

"Seven," he said quietly, all the time staring at Holmes intently.

Arthur spoke up again, "Are you the detective man?" he asked of Holmes.

"Yes," my friend chuckled, "I am the detective man, have you heard of me?"

"Oh yes, my mother reads us your stories, doesn't she Cecil? Don't you Mother?" Arthur replied animatedly.

"Yes, darlings I do," said Mrs. Jacobs.

"I have to say, Mrs. Jacobs, that I am not too sure of the suitability of my stories for minors, they are written with adults in mind and with such themes as murder, extortion and various other crimes, I cannot in all conscience proclaim them as wholesome reading for children," I said, somewhat pompously maybe.

"You may have a point, Dr. Watson and as you are the author it is hardly incumbent in me to argue the point, but I do foresee a time, it may even be fifty years or more hence, when children all over the world will fall in love with the adventures of Sherlock Holmes," Mrs. Jacobs reasoned.

"Adventures! See what you have done, Watson, the science of deduction brought low," said Holmes in evident good humour.

I did my best to ignore Holmes. "You flatter me, Mrs. Jacobs. I very much doubt that Holmes or I will be remembered in the future in spite of my modest efforts to provide us with an immortality of a kind."

Jacobs laughed, "Well, it's no use saying to you both, wait and see!"

While this was going on, a quite extraordinary thing was happening. Holmes was marching around the sitting room with both boys in tow, examining every surface with his magnifying lens before handing it over to them to look through. They were squealing excitedly and enjoying the game of being a master detective. This was far, far removed from the Holmes I knew and it was a delight to see him so relaxed; perhaps this holiday would be beneficial for him after all.

Jacobs explained that they usually had a main meal in the middle of the day, but he would rustle up some cold meats or fish and vegetables to serve as supper if we so desired. We indicated that would be perfectly acceptable and he went, along with his wife, to prepare it. The boys were quite happy playing by themselves and Holmes was perched awkwardly on a chaise-longue, deep in thought.

"A lovely family, don't you think, Holmes?" I ventured.

"Yes, Watson, lovely indeed, but I was just casting my mind back to what Jacobs said regarding curious events."

"It may be nothing, curious can just mean no more than that, an odd event, something out of the commonplace which is soon forgotten when something else takes its place."

"I'm sure you are right, but surely I have to take into account the undeniable fact that you are the stormy petrel of crime," said Holmes, laughing in his familiar, silent manner.

"Really, Holmes, I must protest, crime no more follows me around than it does you, in fact, considerably less so I would say," I replied loftily.

"Well, we will possess our souls in patience until Jacobs favours us with an explanation of his curious events later."

"Very well, Holmes, but please remember this *is* a holiday!" I said.

As Jacobs returned to the room, I was struck by the thought that he was still a handsome man, perhaps even more so than when I first knew him. In those days he was exceedingly popular with the ladies, more so than me as I recall. Even now his brown, bushy hair coupled with a fresh complexion still gave him a youthful countenance and it was hard for me to believe over twenty years had passed since our University and rugby playing days.

"Ah, Watson," he said, "you don't look a day older."

"I was just thinking the same of you my old friend, but in your case with rather more justification," I replied.

"It must be the sea air," he opined. "It works wonders you know."

"Somehow, I always expected you to remain a city doctor; you always seemed so at home there among the masses."

"Well, once I was old friend, once I was. Perhaps our lives haven't quite gone how we planned in those far off days, but I would not trade my life now with anybody; I am the happiest I have ever been," Jacobs said, proudly looking at his wife and children.

"I would echo those sentiments," said I.

"Notwithstanding the loss of my dear wife, you see before you a contented man."

"Well, you have certainly made a name for yourself as well as making Holmes's name known before the public. I trust we can expect some more tales from your pen soon?" Jacobs asked.

"Yes certainly, once I have decided what tales are indeed fit to be read by the public, for some are decidedly not so for various reasons, such as matters of delicacy or privacy," I replied. "Even in some of the tales I have chronicled, I have had to alter times, dates, places and disguise identities for exactly those reasons. I have to admit I confuse myself quite often, I only hope I do not leave the readers in a similar state."

Holmes interrupted our conversation. "Watson usually selects such tales according to their sensationalism, as opposed to emphasising the scientific deductions that have been made in bringing the cases to a successful conclusion. I do despair sometimes I must confess."

"Really, Holmes as I have said to you on many occasions, perhaps you should try putting pen to paper yourself, you then may see the difficulties that have to be overcome. The accounts must contain a modicum of entertainment in order to make them readable for the public."

"I believe you have made a very good point there," said Jacobs.

"Thank you my friend. It is never an easy task to assemble a tale from my notebooks. Holmes always wishes me to show the analytical reasoning behind each link in the case whereas I prefer to show the human element involved."

"Well, Watson, I have to say you have done a very good job indeed," Jacobs said glowingly.

"Thank you, Jacobs."

From the chaise-longue, there came a discreet cough. "I believe you had something to tell us, Dr. Jacobs," said Holmes insistently.

Holmes was accustomed to getting his own way and was crestfallen when Jacobs again put off the regaling of recent events here, in favour of tackling the supper that he and his wife had prepared for us and a fine one it was too. We had only been in

Lyme Regis a few hours and already we had partaken of two excellent meals. Holmes and I were treated to a potted history of Lyme as we ate. Like many towns, Lyme had endured its tragedies; major fires at regular intervals had destroyed portions of the town, in spite of the protection the Cobb offered, storms from the sea had carried away many, many dwellings throughout its long and chequered history. In times of war and crises Lyme was always to the fore, supplying ships and men to combat the Spanish Armada, withstanding a long, drawn out siege during the Civil War and then some forty years later, a great number of townsfolk were to be found siding with the Duke of Monmouth during his unsuccessful rebellion of 1685, some of whom were found guilty of treason by Judge Jeffreys and summarily executed for their allegiance on the very beach where Monmouth had disembarked. As Jacobs spoke, I made mental notes of particular places to visit to fully immerse myself in the history of Lyme Regis.

In due course, Arthur and Cecil were despatched to bed, but not before they had extracted promises from Holmes and myself to visit again, which we were more than happy to do. Mrs. Jacobs, Sarah, joined us in the sitting-room and we relaxed with a glass of Beaune each, tired, all of us at the end of a long day, but none of us quite wanting the evening to end just yet.

"Dr. Jacobs......." prompted Holmes, who was determined not to be denied a third time.

"Yes, the time is right, Mr. Holmes. First of all, you must know that I was not an eye-witness to all I am going to relate to you, so my re-telling may be somewhat disjointed."

"Never fear, Dr. Jacobs, pray begin and please omit no detail, however inconsequential it may seem," Holmes said firmly.

"Really, Holmes, you sound as though you are at the start of an investigation into some vast criminal conspiracy," said I.

"Yes," echoed Jacobs, "I have little to tell you other than oddities, although there is tragedy involved too."

"Please do so then, Doctor," Holmes said, with impatience which bordered on rudeness to my mind.

"Very well," began Jacobs. "The first singular occurrence was in the second week of April, it was a Friday evening not too long before sunset. It had been a fairly calm day, but as the sun began its descent in the sky a terrific gale blew up from nowhere, ships in the harbour were tossed around like children's playthings and huge waves broke over the Cobb and the pier. In the middle of this maelstrom there appeared a schooner, propelled forward by the storm, but witnesses I have spoken to myself, hold the fervent belief that somehow it was the schooner driving the storm forward."

"How patently absurd," I said. "what a ridiculous notion."

"Yes indeed, Watson, "agreed Jacobs. "No doubt a trick of the light, allied to superstitious minds which I must tell you are in abundance here."

Holmes was in a prone position on the chaise-longue, hands in front of him, steepled, with fingertips lightly touching their opposite numbers. He turned to face Jacobs and asked, "Do any witnesses recall seeing the schooner before the storm arose?"

"As far as I know, they didn't, but that in itself means nothing of course, everyone's attention was drawn to the sea with the outbreak of the storm and not necessarily before," Jacobs replied.

"Yes of course," Holmes said. "Forgive my interruption."

"In spite of the adverse conditions, the lifeboat was launched together with five of her crew. The 'Susan Ashley' has been in use for a few years, but she is easy to manoeuvre even in the highest seas I am told. The winds had eased as they reached the stricken ship which was listing to one side, but otherwise seemingly undamaged by the battering it had taken. There were three large rectangular crates bobbing up and down in the sea by the vessel, but apart from that, nothing."

Jacobs replenished our glasses and having filled his own, took a sip and continued, "There were no discernible markings on the schooner; the hull was jet black as indeed was most of the vessel. Two of the lifeboat's crew managed to board the schooner, but found nothing by the way of a log or maps to indicate where it may have come from or, indeed, where it was bound, although it was the considered opinion of those who know such things that it was of Eastern European manufacture."

"Excuse me, Jacobs," said I interrupting this time, "but surely the crew of the schooner would be able to put that matter right."

"Ah, there you have it, Watson.......there was no crew," Jacobs said emphatically.

At this, Holmes sat upright, his eyes shining. "No crew you say, was there any indication as to what had become of them?"

"Not only that, but there was no indication that there had ever been a crew on board the vessel, none of the usual things you would expect to find, clothing or food for instance."

"Have you any idea, Dr. Jacobs how many crew members you would expect to be on such a vessel?" Holmes asked.

"Six, possibly seven, Mr. Holmes," he replied.

"Thank you and yet there was no sign of such a crew, most singular," Holmes said. "Pray, continue your most interesting narrative."

"There was nothing more to be done that night, the 'Susan Ashley' and her crew returned to shore and the excitement was over for the evening. With the dawn and first light there came another surprise, there was no sign of the schooner whatsoever, no flotsam, no jetsam....not a sign that she had ever been there at all."

"I take it you would expect there to be such debris?" Holmes asked.

"Yes certainly."

"What about the large rectangular crates you mentioned?" I asked.

"Ah yes, Watson...the crates did remain as the one sign that the schooner had been in our waters, they had been washed up on the beach, intact, remarkably so from all accounts," Jacobs answered.

"Presumably these singular crates were recovered and examined, what did their contents reveal?" Holmes asked.

"Very little, as they contained earth and earth alone." Jacobs stared pointedly at each of us in turn as he said this.

"Earth?" Holmes and I both exclaimed together.

"Yes, both crates were examined fully in case there was any form of contraband concealed in the soil, but none was found.....only that confounded earth!"

It all seemed fantastic to me, three crates of soil on board a ship with no crew, which then promptly disappeared without a trace. I could make neither head nor tail of it and Holmes was looking distinctly puzzled too.

"Well," Holmes ventured, "it was a curious event you promised us Doctor and you have certainly delivered that, but I fancy there is more to come. What happened to the crates after they had been examined, were they and their contents disposed of?"

"Normally, you would expect that cargo beached in the manner these crates were would be claimed as salvage, but no one seemed in any hurry to claim three crates of soil as their own, perhaps not surprisingly," Jacobs said laughing. Continuing, he said, "Quite naturally the events of that evening were talked about at some length in the town, with some outlandish tales being spun. Some claimed to have seen a figure on board the schooner as it rode the waves, this figure then apparently diving into the sea as the lifeboat approached, is, but one example. After two days or so the talk dwindled away into nothing. On the third day however, events took another singular turn when a stranger turned up claiming the crates as his own!"

"Most intriguing, Doctor," Holmes said. "Please continue."

"The crates were being stored in the bonded warehouse in Cobb hamlet under the supervision of a Mr. Beviss and that particular evening he was just about to lock up as it was getting on towards eight o' clock and the light was fading fast."

Holmes interrupted again. "Was that his usual finishing time, it seems a trifle late to me although I am willing to be educated on that point?"

"I am not too sure on that myself, but if you wish I am sure Mr. Beviss would be only too glad to confirm the fact for you should you have need of him to do so," Jacobs said helpfully. " To continue, the stranger was a striking individual by all accounts; tall, bald-headed with sharply defined features and peculiarly penetrating eyes and dressed in a long black silken cloak which reached down to his feet. He announced himself to Beviss as Count Orlana, a nobleman from Transylvania, and said the crates were his property, adding that they had been shipped from his homeland via the port of Constantza on the Black Sea."

"Did he offer any documentation to support this claim?" Holmes asked, "or indeed, shed any light on the vessel being apparently crew less, or the origins of it?"

"None at all as far as I am aware, but as the crates only contained earth the usual formalities were dispensed with and he was allowed to take possession. He could shed no light on the schooner and its lack of a crew; the shipping arrangements were made through a third party he explained. The crates were duly loaded onto a cart with the assistance of Mr. Beviss and two particularly menacing looking men that this Count had brought along with him."

At this point I interjected and asked, "Why did he not travel on the schooner himself I wonder?"

"Possibly he was already here and the arrangements were made from this country," Holmes mused. "In any case we have insufficient data to draw any conclusions. Did he offer any reasons for needing these three crates of earth by the way?"

"I believe he mentioned that he was hoping to cultivate a plant from his native Transylvania and had shipped the soil over because it would only grow in that particular type of earth," Jacobs answered.

"I wonder whether that information was a reply to a question, or if it was volunteered?" Holmes said to himself more than to us

"Does it make a difference?" I asked.

"Most assuredly, yes. Well, Dr. Jacobs, it is a most intriguing account you have furnished us with, it presents many points of interest and suggests to me certain paths which may need to be followed. Interestingly, it also reminds me of another happening along the lines that you have described to us, but the details escape me momentarily. I think, good doctors, we may be in very deep waters indeed," Holmes said gravely.

CHAPTER SIX

"**D**o you really think so, Holmes?" I asked. "I know there are certainly oddities in what we have heard, but surely no more than that."

"More than oddities surely, my friend, there are mysteries too. Why no crew members on the schooner? How does the vessel then disappear so utterly? If the ship was blown in by the storm by accident, then how are we to account for the presence of Count Orlana? If, as he says, he knew nothing about the shipping arrangements, then how could he know of its arrival here if it came here by misadventure? If the Count was already here as I assume him to have been and Lyme was indeed the intended destination then how do we account for a ship without a crew sailing into the harbour?" Holmes demanded of us.

"But," I ventured, "the ship was blown in, rather than being sailed in. Perhaps the crew were thrown overboard in their efforts to keep the vessel on an even keel and a sudden squall in the early hours may have finished it off."

"Your theory has a lot to recommend it my dear fellow, but does not explain the absence of debris or bodies, my knowledge of tides is somewhat lacking, but I would certainly expect bodies to be washed up on the beach within a day or two at most and definitely in the vicinity of the bay itself. Also you remember, those of the lifeboat crew who boarded the schooner reported no indication that there had ever been a crew," replied Holmes.

I clung on to the remnants of my theory with an ever loosening grip. "But that was only a quick search to ascertain whether there was anybody on board. It is possible that there were signs of habitation which were missed, after all it was sunset and the light would have almost gone."

"Yes, Watson I concede that point to you, for it is unthinkable that the schooner came here from the shores of the Black Sea under its own steam and so the probability is that there was a crew and that they met their end shortly before the end of the voyage. As to what that end may have been, I cannot say. God rest their souls."

"Tell me, Dr. Jacobs," Holmes asked, "was there any form of official investigation into the disappearance of this unidentified schooner?"

"There was, I believe, no basis on which to conduct such an investigation. The only physical signs left of the schooner were of course the three crates. Enquiries were made with the usual authorities regarding overdue or missing vessels, but nothing corresponded with the vessel that had been sighted in our waters."

"And Count Orlana? Is there any news on his whereabouts?"

"Yes, he is still here in Lyme Regis. He has taken up residence at Haye Manor. It is the home of Sir Peter Rattenbury, but he is travelling in Italy until at least the autumn. I do not know what connection there may be between the Count and Sir Peter howbeit there is no reason for me to know. Sir Peter is a renowned expert on Eastern Europe and he may have possibly met the Count on his travels, or perhaps they have corresponded."

"Thank you; the connection can remain a matter for conjecture. At least now we know the schooner came here, not by accident, but by design," Holmes pronounced.

We both looked expectantly at Jacobs for we knew there was more to come and he did not disappoint us. He rose to his feet and pulled his chair closer to ours, almost in a conspiratorial manner and seating himself again, he continued, "We now come to the 'Black Dog of Lyme'," he said. "Along with many other parts of the country we have a so called 'Black Dog'; our dog haunts a particular lane, Haye Lane. I won't vex you with the provenance of the tale, but it a well known old legend and runs pretty much in line with all of these tales; a jet black dog with eyes of red crossing the path of unsuspecting God-fearing folk and scaring them to Kingdom come. I call it legend, but there have been numerous sightings over the last few weeks, not just in Haye Lane, but throughout the town."

"Hysteria," said I, "someone imagines they see something of the supernatural in a perfectly ordinary dog, for whatever reason and before you know it everyone is seeing the blessed thing, I have come across this sort of thing many times before."

"Ordinarily I would agree with you, but many of these sightings have been reported by respectable people, professional people, pillars of the community you might say," Jacobs said kindly.

"And when exactly, did *you* see the dog, Dr. Jacobs?" Holmes inquired.

Jacobs laughed, "Bravo.....yes I did see the dog and it was as real to me as either one of you."

Mrs. Jacobs, who had been intent on some embroidery in the corner of the room, spoke up, "What a sight he was when he burst through the door, white as a sheet and hair standing up on end.I have never seen my husband looks so scared, gentlemen."

"Yes, Sarah is right, I was certainly scared, I don't mind admitting it," Jacobs said. "I had been to see a patient in Colway Lane and was walking back down the lane towards the river. I had just passed the old manor house when a large black dog burst through the hedge directly into my path."

"You say through, but could it just have easily been over, perchance?" Holmes asked.

"I had the distinct impression it was through. The unreality of the situation struck me when I realised it had done so with no discernible sound whatsoever. It was massive, the largest dog I have ever seen and it turned to face me with the reddest of eyes staring straight into my own. I felt unable to move for those few seconds and then it was gone, bounding away up the lane towards Haye Manor."

"Haye Manor? Sir Peter Rattenbury's home, yes?"

"Yes, Mr. Holmes, is it of any importance?"

"Merely a fact that can be docketed away, it may later prove to have a bearing on matters," Holmes replied. "Please continue."

"I am not a man given to fancies, but for those short few moments I was under its spell entirely and felt drained of all my energy. And, ahem, there is one more thing," he said, seemingly somewhat reluctant to speak of it.

"Yes?" Holmes asked.

"Now, forgive me, for this really is fanciful, it appeared to speak to me."

"Speak!" I exclaimed.

"Yes, Watson my old friend, speak, but how can I explain without seeming to you both a madman; I heard the voice in my head only. It seemed to me it said something along the lines of 'you would make a good enemy'."

"Extraordinary. What a very singular thing to have happened," Holmes said and none of us in that small sitting room could possibly gainsay that. "Was that the only occasion you encountered this remarkable beast?"

"Believe me, Mr. Holmes, once was more than enough for this man, I had no wish or desire to have a further encounter."

"As far as you know, did others encounter this dog in much the same circumstances as yourself, Doctor?" Holmes inquired.

"I believe so, Mr. Holmes, although I cannot say for sure."

"And did you form an opinion as to whether you were seeing a spectral beast or one of flesh and blood?" Holmes asked.

"Apart from its great size, it seemed a normal dog. It appeared to be entirely solid and yet all my senses told me that I was seeing something other worldly, loathe as I was to admit such a thing."

"And what do you make of it all?" Holmes asked of him.

"I really cannot say," Jacobs answered. "The logician in me says these things are connected, but I cannot quite see how or, indeed, why."

"Perhaps it may yet become clear to us. You mentioned a tragedy earlier I believe, Doctor," Holmes said, leaning forward with a most earnest look on his face.

"Yes," he said grimly. "A young girl who wasted away and died at the tender age of eighteen, her name was Rose Hannington. She lived with her parents and her cousin Elizabeth at Silver Lodge which is situated on a small lane just off the road to Axminster. In fact, you would have passed very close to the house in question on your journey to Lyme earlier today. Rose was taken ill a little over two weeks ago, an illness that so sapped her strength that she succumbed only a few days later."

"How many days, Doctor?"

"I believe it was in the region of a week, Mr. Holmes," Jacobs replied.

"Thank you. Were you not her physician then?" Holmes asked.

"No, as the residence in question was over the border into Devonshire, it fell to Dr. Pomphlett to treat her. He is a most able doctor, rather behind the times maybe, but he is well respected in the community."

"Where does Dr. Pomphlett reside?" interrupted Holmes.

"In Uplyme."

"A local man then. Did he ask you for your opinion regarding the girl?"

"No, it is this way Mr. Holmes, he has his patients and I have mine and we are not given to discussing them on the social occasions when we meet save for those that perhaps display some singular features."

"Did the illness of Rose Hannington display enough singular features for Dr. Pomphlett to discuss her sickness with you?" Holmes asked.

"Yes, Mr. Holmes, but only after the sad event."

"I see, no doubt though, you are aware of his diagnosis of this particular illness?"

"Yes he attributed it to a form of anaemia, a particularly virulent form. More than that I cannot say, no doubt Pomphlett could give you more details concerning what course of action was taken to halt this illness. It would normally take the form of extra vitamins or iron tablets which can reverse the symptoms. In spite of his ministrations, Rose died."

"Did the doctor form an opinion as to the origins of this sudden illness?"

"No, he was unable to account for it."

"Are there occasional diseases brought in by foreign sailors, it can often be the way in port towns?" Holmes asked.

"It is not unknown certainly, but as far as I know Rose was not one for visiting the harbour, in fact she led a quiet life at home to the best of my knowledge."

"Well, it is a very sad tale indeed, but I fancy, Doctor there is still some further embellishment to this story," Holmes opined.

"Here again, gentlemen, you must be prepared to suspend belief as I have been. Rose has been seen since her death, both in the cemetery grounds and in the lanes which lead from Silver Lodge to the eastern side of town."

"Would Haye Lane be involved perchance? And precisely who has seen her?" Holmes asked.

"Why yes, Haye Lane is indeed one of the lanes in question and at least eight people have reported seeing her apparition, three of those who have seen her to my certain knowledge knew her very well and are unlikely to be mistaken in their identification, but again, there is yet more to this," Jacobs answered.

I could scarcely take in what I had been hearing. The whole town seemed to be in the grip of a monstrous malady, mysterious shipwrecks, an equally mysterious nobleman and phantoms of dogs and girls abounding, my mind raced to make a connection between all of this, but I was left floundering. Just what had been happening in this town? So deep was I in thought that I had missed Jacobs's words as he began to speak again. "Sorry, old friend, I was lost in my thoughts for a moment," I said.

"Don't worry about it, old chap, there has certainly been a lot to take in tonight. I have been puzzling over it for some time, but I was saying, there is more to this. Just three days ago, a Victor Selby encountered the apparition of Rose Hannington on Horn Bridge on Colway Lane. Now, you must know that Victor and

Rose were the same age and virtually grew up together. Indeed, at one time they were sweethearts. Victor swears to anyone who will listen, that Rose called to him. In spite of the fact he knew she was no more on this earth, he went to her, whereupon she embraced him. He was powerless to resist, she held him tight, then he says he felt her teeth puncture his neck, at this he recovered his senses and pushing her away with all his might, he ran for home as fast as he could."

"Extraordinary, what are your opinions regarding this matter, Doctor, do you accept that these people, young Selby included have actually encountered the spirit of Rose Hannington?"

"I do not believe the dead walk the earth, Mr. Holmes, either the witnesses have been mistaken in what they have seen or a cruel trick is being perpetrated here, how and to what end I confess I cannot begin to guess."

"Well, Watson," Holmes said smiling. "You have brought me to a most exceptional place, where ghosts and phantoms would appear to be habitual."

"No laughing matter surely," I rejoined testily.

"No, it is not my friend, it is a very serious matter and to be frank, I am at a loss how to proceed."

"But what is there to proceed with? We can hardly call Lestrade down from Scotland Yard to arrest a phantom no matter what crimes it may have committed. I still think my mass hysteria has some bearing on the matter," I averred.

"You may well be right my dear fellow, I certainly have no other theory to offer at the moment although as I say, I have a vague recollection of something similar occurring in...........no matter, it has fled from me, perhaps a good night's rest will refresh my memory."

"Well, Dr. Jacobs, you have given us a very full account of all that has happened here of late, how did you come by all your information may I ask?"

"It is a small town, Mr. Holmes with long tongues and news travels quickly as though it has wings."

Time had passed quickly and I was surprised at the lateness of the hour. I was very aware that neither Holmes nor I had a key to Mrs. Heidler's establishment so that we would have no recourse but to disturb her to gain admittance. I was selfish in my thoughts I must admit, because I was very much looking forward to seeing her again no matter how late the hour was.

"One question before we go," I said to Jacobs. "I presume Victor is one of your patients, did you examine his neck for the wound he described?"

"An excellent question, my boy," Holmes said. "Well, Jacobs?"

"All I could see was a slight discolouration, nothing to indicate a bite or puncture. Although let me say I strongly and firmly believe in the veracity of the account that Victor rendered, when I treated him he was clearly still much shaken."

"Thank you, Doctor, will you also indulge me in one more question, in your correspondence with Watson, you did not mention any of these events, why?"

"I hardly saw the need," he answered Holmes bluntly. "I was inviting Watson down for a holiday, not to hunt ghosts and phantoms down and besides the more mysterious of these events have occurred quite recently."

"I see.....well, thank you and good night, Doctor. It has been a most illuminating evening and good night, Mrs. Jacobs, thank you for your hospitality."

"Good night, Mr. Holmes, good night, Dr. Watson," Mrs. Jacobs called.

"Well, well, that was quite a tale your friend Jacobs had to tell," Holmes said, as we stepped out into Sherborne Lane, "don't you think, Watson?"

"Yes indeed, Holmes. I confess I have no idea what to make of it all. You recall hearing about a similar event elsewhere you mentioned I believe?"

"Yes, but for the life of me I cannot recall where or even when, no matter, I have no doubt it will come to me."

We walked down the lane the few yards into Coombe Street, the moon and stars were shining brightly. On a lovely night like this, it was hard to conceive of a world in which spectres and revenants walked, if indeed they did. I was quite sure all the witnesses to the phantoms in Lyme would swear as to what they had seen, yet I was not convinced of it, at least not entirely. We arrived at Mrs. Heidler's in no time at all. The door was opened very swiftly by the lady herself. "Good evening gentlemen, I trust you have had an agreeable time?" she asked, with just the merest hint of admonishment in her voice.

"Yes thank you, Mrs. Heidler, a most agreeable time and we must apologise for the lateness of the hour, we were simply unaware of how the time had passed, please forgive us," I said.

"Oh, come now, there is no need for you be worrying about that, I was more than content sitting by the fire, reading."

"Thank you, you are most gracious, may I ask what you were reading?"

"Oh, nothing really, an old magazine that was lying around, it passed the time," she replied.

"Well we will bid you good night then," I said. As we walked towards the stairs I looked down to the small table by the fire where there lay an old copy of 'The Strand.' A flush of pleasure ran through me as I noticed it was one containing one of the adventures that Holmes and I had been involved in.

"Good night gentlemen, breakfast will be ready for nine-thirty unless you are in need earlier."

We agreed that nine-thirty would be entirely agreeable and retired to our rooms. I was yawning all the way up those rickety stairs and knew that Morpheus would soon claim me as one of his own, whereas I was positive that Holmes would be up all night, mulling over what he had heard this evening and trying to reason out in his mind exactly what was going on here.

I bade Holmes good night and only a few minutes later my head merely brushed the pillow and I was asleep.

I awoke rather later than intended, but still in ample time for breakfast. I attended to my toilet and dressed myself in a new set of tweeds which had caught my eye whilst visiting my tailors in Oxford Street, shortly before our departure to Lyme Regis. I rapped on Holmes's door as I went by, but received no reply. Mrs. Heidler was in the parlour and most pleasingly, complimented me on my appearance. "Tweeds really do something for a man, don't you think, Dr. Watson?" she asked me, almost in a coquettish manner.

"I am rather hoping that is the case, my dear lady," I countered.

She laughed and showed me through to a small room to the rear of the parlour where we were to eat. Nathaniel was there busying himself laying a table for two. I received a grunt as a riposte to my good morning greeting, which I translated as a reciprocal good morning. There was no sign of Holmes and Mrs. Heidler had not seen him, but she had heard the front door opening and closing an hour or so before. Barely a minute later Nathaniel went to answer a knocking at the door and Holmes strode into the room. "Hullo stay-a-bed Watson, the best of the day is gone already my boy. I have had a most invigorating walk, my lungs are full of the freshest of air and I am ready to devour breakfast in its entirety."

"Must you be so insufferably cheery in the morning, Holmes? It is positively inhuman of you sometimes," I said, with a broad smile on my face.

"Now then, Watson, have you given any more thought to the singular and curious happenings as described to us by your friend?"

"My first thought was not a very charitable one, it was; what ineffable twaddle all this talk of ghosts and spirits is and as yet, I have to say my thinking has not moved on from this stance."

"You certainly cannot be blamed for thinking that way and yet, although I would like to side with you, I do believe there is something at work here and there is both rhyme and reason to what has been seen and heard. Alas, we have yet to ascertain what that could be."

"You surprise me, Holmes. I think of you as the most flat-footed of men, one who is committed to the science of reason not to chasing ghosts and phantoms."

"I am not particularly well up on my Shakespeare, Watson as you know, but I think it was Hamlet who said, '*There are more things in heaven and earth Horatio, than are dreamt of in your philosophy.*' Act 1. Scene V. I believe. I commend it to us both as good advice to keep our minds truly open and receptive."

"Have you still not managed to recall where you have heard about such happenings before, Holmes?"

"Yes, Watson, I have to say that most of the account has come back to me, but I am unsure as to its relevance to events here, yet.........ah food!"

Breakfast was then upon us and I have to report that we did full justice to it. Holmes was exceedingly garrulous and we discoursed at length on various subjects. We also discussed our plans for the day, I had none fixed, save for visiting one or two of the sites Jacobs mentioned that pertained to the history of Lyme and maybe to walk into the surrounding countryside. Holmes was planning to collect some fossils and study the local geology as well as taking in the exhibition of William Buckland's work at the Victoria Hall. We agreed to go our separate ways and to catch up with each other later in the day. Within seconds Holmes was gone.

I often find myself prone to fits of extreme idleness and I was in no hurry at all to start my day, this place positively encouraged such laziness! And who was I to argue against it?

David Ruffle

CHAPTER SEVEN

Nathaniel cleared away the remnants of breakfast whilst I sought out Mrs. Heidler to thank her for the most splendid meal; it had set me up for the day wonderfully. I found her in the scullery, with arms deep in a sink full of suds, scrubbing pans. "Thank you, Mrs. Heidler for the most welcome breakfast, it was a nourishing and delicious way to start the day," said I.

"It was my pleasure, Dr. Watson; I like to see that all my guests have a hearty breakfast. To my mind it is the most important meal of the day, don't you agree?"

"Yes, indeed I do, I have always advocated the importance of it to my patients."

"Have you plans for today, Doctor?"

"I learned a little more about the history of Lyme Regis yesterday evening from my friend Dr. Jacobs and it is my intention to have a walking tour taking in many of the places he mentioned........he also....." I faltered here, not sure whether to bring the matter up; taking a deep breath, I continued, "he also mentioned the small matter of ghosts and spectres which have been seen recently in the vicinity of both Haye Lane and Colway Lane. I thought I may take in those two places also."

"There has been strange activity here of late right enough. Nathaniel says he is always very wary these days if out in the dark," said Mrs. Heidler, then laughed, "in all honesty though, Lyme is no stranger to ghosts that's for sure. Who knows, you may meet Judge Jeffreys or the Duke of Monmouth on your walk!?"

I laughed too, "Who knows, dear lady, who knows!?"

"Will you and Mr. Holmes be requiring an evening meal, Doctor? If so, it will be early, at five-thirty."

"I am sure that will be eminently suitable. Indeed, I was hoping to dine early on account of the Grand Dance that is to be held in the Assembly Rooms tonight, I have a mind to attend."

"Do you dance then, Dr. Watson?" Mrs. Heidler asked of me.

"Oh, just a little," I rejoined. "And even then, I have to confess, a trifle clumsily."

"Oh, surely not," she exclaimed.

"I am afraid so Mrs. Heidler."

"Oh well, the dances are usually splendid occasions. I am confident you will find it most enjoyable."

"You have been yourself no doubt then?"

"Yes, when certain gentlemen of the town have requested my company, such as it is."

"I have no doubt that your company is worthy of any grand occasion. Has your company been requested for this evening's occasion perchance?"

"It has not, Doctor. I fear approaching middle-age has curtailed such invitations," she said, smiling.

"Very well then, would you do me the signal honour of accompanying me to this evening's dance?"

"Why, Dr. Watson, if you are sure, it would be a pleasure to do so, thank you."

We stood there smiling at each other a little awkwardly until I said I must fetch my cap from my room and start on my little tour.

I stepped out with a light heart and no clear idea of where to start. As the events recounted yesterday evening were still fresh in my mind, I sought out the two lanes in question. By following the path of the River Lym upstream, a most picturesque walk I must add, I soon came to Horn Bridge where Victor Selby had such a dramatic confrontation with his former sweetheart. The path here was in a narrow valley with a steep climb to my left, also to my right. If I had my bearings correct then Colway Lane was the road to my right. I turned that way firstly and walked the length of the lane until it connected with the road to Bridport. It was an arduous climb and my old wound was reminding me of its existence.

As Haye Lane was in the opposite direction, there was nothing for it, but to descend the way I had just come. There were very few dwellings here, but I caught sight of what must be the old manor house that Jacobs had mentioned. It looked somewhat dilapidated and uncared for, how sad I thought that such grand houses which have seen so much life and had so much life lived in them should end up this way; neglected. I retraced my steps to Horn Bridge and after resting for a few moments I began another ascent, thankfully much shorter this time, up to Haye Lane.

Haye Manor was on my right, an imposing house, late Tudor I thought with its red brick facade so redolent of the period. I wondered whether Count Orlana was in there as I watched, maybe poring over his boxes of earth, impelling his plants to take hold. My daydreaming was brought to an abrupt end by a shout in my direction. Coming towards me was a rough looking fellow striding purposefully. Long before he came near to me, he was shouting, "Hey, you there, get away...this is private property see."

"My good man, I was merely admiring the building, there is no need whatsoever for the tone in your voice," I remonstrated.

He was now directly in front of me, he had long black hair, unwashed, unkempt and a mean narrow-lipped mouth. He snarled at me, "I am not your good man see........now be off with you and admire another damned building."

"Your behaviour is outrageous sir," I spluttered.

"Yes isn't it? Now clear off or I will set the dogs on you."

"I have a good mind to report you to the local constabulary, ordinary folk going about their own business should not be threatened in such a manner by the likes of you."

"Go to the constabulary or go to hell, it is all the same to me," with that he turned and strode away in the direction of the house.

How extraordinary I thought, was he acting under orders from Count Orlana to keep visitors away? And if so: why?

Shaking my head, I regained my composure and carried on up Haye Lane to where it met the road to Axminster. I turned towards Lyme and immediately passed the Black Dog Inn, another connection with the old legend so recently brought to life in mysterious fashion. I mused on this....was this black dog, perhaps not a ghostly one, but a large breed made to appear frightening by some means of artificially reddening the eyes? And all of this to ensure people would be kept away from Haye Manor. After all, I thought, the recent sightings have all coincided with the arrival of this extraordinary sounding Count Orlana in Lyme Regis. Perhaps the apparition of Rose was also something of the kind, a decoy of sorts. Maybe a servant who was masquerading as the departed Rose? For it struck me that for this spectre of Rose to sink her teeth into young Victor as she held him, then surely she must be a creature of flesh and blood. I resolved to bring this reasoning to the attention of Holmes when I next saw him.

My route back into Lyme was now fortunately downhill. As I descended I tried to imagine for myself the scene when Lyme was besieged in 1644, with the Royalist army firing down cannonballs and flaming arrows into the town for nine long weeks. I looked around scanning the surroundings, trying to work out where the Royalists may have set up their gun placements. Though heavily outnumbered, the defence held firm and the army commanded by Prince Maurice had to withdraw, with heavy losses too from all accounts. One of the things I had gleaned from the history of Lyme I had perused on the journey here was that it had a fiercely independent spirit in all things. Whether it was politics or religion, the people of Lyme usually managed to take a different slant on matters and sometimes suffered for it.

By now I found myself at the top of Broad Street where all the buildings seemed to be in a veritable hurry to rush down towards the sea. I stopped off at Beer and Sons the tobacconist to replenish my dwindling stock of Ships' tobacco and then marched on down the hill. I looked in at the Victoria Hall to see if Holmes was there attending the exhibition, there was no sign of him however. I elected to stay for a few moments examining some of the exhibits. There were many, many copies of Buckland's work on Geology and Mineralogy, bones and fossils were also in abundance. I must admit I found the whole thing rather dry and not very involving. The only thing I could really recall about Buckland was his claim to have eaten his way through the entire animal kingdom, it was not reported how the animal kingdom felt about it!

I headed out towards Monmouth beach, which lies directly behind the Cobb. This was where the Duke had landed in June of 1685 to commence his plan to usurp the throne from his uncle, James. Lyme had been chosen by the Duke for its Protestant sympathies. Many local folk had heeded the call and joined up with this charismatic figure. Defeat came all too predictably to the Duke and his untrained army at the battle of Sedgemoor. Reprisals were swift and bloody. Ninety nine men of Lyme were arrested and twelve met their grisly end atop a scaffold on the beach where Monmouth had landed a short while before. The Duke himself suffered a botched execution in July the same year on Tower Hill.

"Yes, Watson, a sad end indeed," said a familiar voice.

"This time, Holmes, I have no need to ask you how you deduced my thoughts. I am quite sure my face betrayed my feelings only too well."

"Your features are your faithful servants, Watson, as always," Holmes said.

Holmes's pockets were bulging and almost overflowing.

"What have you there, fossils?" I inquired.

"Yes, quite a pretty collection I must say. What did you think of the exhibition of William Buckland's life and work?"

"How on earth did you know I had been there, did you observe me?"

"No, but I observe you now and you have some red dust adhering to the left instep of your left boot, there was a quantity of such dust in the entrance of the hall, elementary, Watson."

"Evidently, Holmes."

"What say you, shall we take some refreshment old fellow?"

"A capital idea," I readily agreed.

We adjourned to the Volunteer Arms at the top of Broad Street where we enjoyed an extremely fine crab sandwich apiece. Holmes sampled the local ale, whereas I was enticed by the smell of a locally produced cider. I inquired of the landlord whether it was supposed to look that cloudy, thinking perhaps it had gone off in the spring warmth, but his look and laugh told me otherwise. The taste however, was exquisite. As we were sitting there, I apprised Holmes on my singular encounter outside Haye Manor and also my theory regarding the apparitions seen in the vicinity thereof.

"Yes, that much had occurred to me already," was his simple reply.

"Oh," I said, feeling a little put out that my own line of thought had been dismissed so.

"No, no, Watson, do not be down, your reasoning was well thought out and entirely sound. I sometimes feel that in your written accounts, you habitually underestimate your own part in our small adventures in order to elevate my own, please be assured that I could never wish for a more able and intelligent assistant and loyal, trustworthy friend."

My heart seemed to swell with pleasure at these words, especially as I was so rarely the recipient of Holmes's approbation. "Thank you, Holmes," barely able to conceal the emotion in my voice, "thank you, in my dual capacity as comrade and friend, you can always count on me to be by your side."

"This I know, Watson, thank you my friend. I believe I will spend the afternoon trying to unravel the mysteries of the Dorset dialect."

"Not our present mysteries, Holmes?" I asked.

"Not unless some criminal activity should present itself in connection with those mysteries, no, Watson."

"Young Selby was attacked, remember."

"As Jacobs intimated, there was no clear evidence of such an attack and if there were, Selby would be willing to swear it was a spectre which carried out the attack which rather takes it out of our jurisdiction my boy."

"Then there is the mystery of the missing crew too," I continued.

"True, but again, nothing at this stage to indicate felonious activity, so, I fear it will have to be the mysteries of language for me, just as abstruse as any puzzles which have happened to come our way in the past."

My own plans for the afternoon consisted of nothing more than purchasing a newspaper and seating myself next to the harbour whilst I read it, so we once again went our separate ways after I had remembered to tell Holmes that the evening meal was set for five-thirty. I had a most agreeable afternoon, reading my newspaper and watching the comings and goings in the small harbour. Well before five I strolled back to Coombe Street to enable me to dress in plenty of time for dinner. I have to admit to being quite excited about the evening ahead. I was looking forward immensely to Mrs. Heidler's company and fervently hoped she was feeling the same about the prospect of spending the evening with me. I reprimanded myself for being so fanciful, it was just a dance, yet when she smiled at me, I felt it was somehow more than just a smile. There had been no intimations nor inclinations of romance since my beautiful Mary had passed away and even now I felt pangs of guilt for merely allowing such thoughts to enter my head. I dressed deep in thought with mixed emotions battling inside me and descended the stairs with a heavier heart than when I had ascended them.

Holmes was already seated at the table, albeit still in his outdoor clothes. There was a heavenly aroma of pork and almost at once Mrs. Heidler brought in two dishes of pork chops garnished with fried slices of apple, together with an ample array of vegetables. It was once again splendid fare. During the meal I announced to Holmes that I would be attending the dance at the Assembly Rooms and invited him to join me. Not surprisingly he declined my invitation to attend, but stated it was his intention to study and catalogue his collection of fossils and to copy out the contents of his notebook, which was now full of examples of the idiosyncrasies and peculiarities of the local dialect. These he hoped would help him to establish that supposed link to those early Phoenician traders and the first settlers in Lyme he had earlier spoken of. I excused myself and returned to my room to ready myself for the evening.

I came down just over an hour later to find Mrs. Heidler in the parlour, dressed in a lovely gown of peacock blue with silken leg of mutton sleeves. I have to say I thought the gown very décolleté, yet looked on the lady in question with great pleasure. "My dear lady, you look radiant, I should say I will be the envy of many a gentleman of Lyme this evening."

"Why, thank you, Doctor," she said, blushing slightly, "and I am equally sure that many a lady present tonight will look on me with envy too."

We walked the short distance from Coombe Street to the Assembly Rooms arm in arm. It was a fine, clear evening. The sun was still shining, albeit weakly in the western firmament. There was neither a cloud in the sky nor in my heart. All I felt was rapture; rapture at being here in this beautiful place and also with so lovely a companion. The whole of the highest social strata of Lyme appeared to be in attendance, all dressed in their finery. Music was playing as we walked into the surprisingly spacious ballroom. I could see four musicians, three playing violins and one a violoncello. At the far end was a huge bay window which looked directly out to sea, giving a most pleasing panoramic view of the bay. Indeed, perched as the rooms were, somewhat precariously to my mind right above the sea, it felt for all the world as though we were afloat. The lamps around the perimeter of the ball room were reflected overhead in three huge chandeliers, aiding a most agreeable atmosphere. Dancing was not the only activity on offer; there were ante-rooms where the men folk could play billiards or cards, also a small reading room where there were at least five newspapers for everyone to peruse the latest news, of both a national and local nature.

Mrs. Heidler, not sparing my blushes, introduced me to all and sundry as 'the famous Dr.Watson' and everyone was most eager for news of Holmes, there had been rumours he was here with me, I was told. Was he here with me? Was he working on a case? I replied that he was indeed here, but only in the capacity of a holiday maker and not as a sleuth. Little did I know that only a few hours later we would find ourselves embroiled in the darkest of mysteries, the like of which I had never known.

The evening has passed into my memory as a simply marvellous occasion. Mrs. Heidler and I danced many a waltz and although I have a natural self-consciousness and reticence regarding public displays of rhythm, I believe I acquitted myself reasonably well. I stopped short of dancing the polka however; it was precisely the kind of energetic activity my old wound protested at vehemently. During the final dance of the evening my beautiful companion laughed and said, "Just think, Doctor Watson, Jane Austen herself would have danced in these rooms and who knows, perhaps on this very spot."

"It is a very pleasant thought admittedly," I said.

"Why, if you had been here ninety or so years ago, you could have danced with the lady herself, wouldn't that have been delightful?"

"My dear lady," I exclaimed, "I could not possibly see how Miss Austen's company could have been more delightful than your own."

All too soon that final dance came to an end, I retrieved my coat and Mrs. Heidler's cloak, bade various good nights and we stepped out into the mild Spring night. We walked back to Coombe Street, again arm in arm. "Thank you for your most delightful company," I ventured, "I have had a simply wonderful time."

"And I too," she replied. "It was so kind of you to invite me, Doctor. I cannot recall ever having a better time at one of these dances."

"I am pleased to hear you say so," I enthused.

Mrs.Heidler excused herself when we arrived back at the guest house, needing to retire so as to be up beforetime tomorrow. I thanked her again, kissed her proffered hand and retired, myself. I intended to say good night to Holmes, but there was no light shining from his room so I passed straight into my own. As I made ready for bed, I picked up my watch which held a locket on its chain, the locket contained a picture of my poor Mary. As I gazed on her likeness, I became at once moved by feelings of guilt that I had enjoyed so much the company of another woman. "Forgive me Mary," I whispered in the dark and the tears began to flow. I tossed and turned and thought sleep would never come whilst private battles raged in me, but eventually I dropped off only to be rudely awoken some hours later by Holmes and news which would plunge us headfirst into an adventure, an adventure which would bring us face to face with unimaginable evil and so very nearly cost us our lives.

CHAPTER EIGHT

Distantly in my sleep, I registered the tapping on the door and when that failed to rouse me completely, Holmes flung the door open wide and bellowed in my direction, "Watson, Watson! Dr. Jacobs is in need of our assistance...come now."

"Whatever is it, Holmes?"

"The game is afoot once more my dear fellow. Do hurry. Five minutes, Watson, five minutes," he shouted as he rushed down the stairs.

During the course of my fifteen years association with Sherlock Holmes I had become somewhat accustomed to such interruptions to my daily routine. I dressed hurriedly and was downstairs before the five minutes had elapsed.

"Ah, Watson, good man, Jacobs will fill us in on the way," Holmes said.

"On the way to where, Holmes?"

"The beach, dear fellow, the beach!" he answered as though it was the most natural thing to be doing at this hour.

Jacobs explained to us as we hurried along, that he had been woken by a boy sent to him by the local sergeant of police. All he knew for sure was that there had been a body discovered on the sand, foul play was suspected and the doctor's presence was needed to confirm that life was extinct and to hopefully uncover the cause of death. We hurried down to the beach. On our arrival we found two local police officers overseeing the sad scene. Sergeant Quick and Constable Street were introduced to us and expressed no undue surprise at our presence. "We have heard of your doings of course Mr. Holmes and we are right glad to have you here," said Sergeant Quick.

"Thank you, Sergeant," Holmes said.

The body lay at their feet, some twenty-five yards from the eastern wall of the harbour. It was that of a man, completely naked. The cause of death looked simple enough to ascertain. He had an horrific wound to the neck; the skin had been torn away savagely in the area of the jugular vein. He had a peculiarly shrivelled look, something I had not previously seen in any corpse I had encountered.

"Tell me, gentlemen," Holmes asked, "when was the body discovered?"

Constable Street was the first to answer, "No more than half an hour ago sir, by a gentleman who happened by whilst walking his dog."

"I take it the body has not been moved or otherwise disturbed?" Holmes asked.

"No sir," said Quick this time, "everything is just as it was," adding, "Inspector Baddeley from Bridport has been wired and is expected to arrive soon and take over the investigation."

"Have you formed a theory yourselves, gentlemen, as to what has occurred here?" Holmes inquired.

"We have not come across the like of this before sir, maybe the gentleman was swimming and was attacked by a marine animal," said Quick.

"Know you of such an animal which can inflict such damage?" Holmes asked.

Street answered, "To be honest, no sir, although all things are possible we reckon."

"If such an attack took place, our friend here did remarkably well to drag himself out of the sea, if indeed he had been in the sea, with such an awful injury as this and up on to the beach whilst neglecting to leave any trails of blood, but as you say, Constable, all things are possible," Holmes countered.

"Perhaps, sir, the outgoing tide has washed away all such evidence," opined the sergeant.

"I think not, I fear we must look elsewhere for a solution. Do either of you know the gentleman?"

"No sir, can't say as we do," Constable Street answered.

"Watson, I take it that I am right in assuming this unfortunate fellow is not one of our elusive crew members?"

"Definitely not, Holmes. I can see no sign that he has been in the water at all," I replied, "besides, the schooner disappeared some weeks ago."

"Just as I thought. Have you an estimate for the time of death?" Holmes asked me.

I glanced at Jacobs who was still examining the body. "I would say around three hours, that would be my best guess without conducting a thorough examination, Mr. Holmes."

Holmes mused to himself, "Before sun up then."

Jacobs called me over to show me something of which he had found, whilst Holmes paced around the scene, occasionally flinging himself to the ground, his eagle eyes having spotted some clue or other. I walked over to him and took him to one side, "Holmes, listen, it is the considered opinion of Jacobs and myself that this man has been exsanguinated. The post-mortem will I think confirm our findings."

"Exsanguinated? Are you saying this poor soul has been drained of blood?" Holmes cried.

"I am saying precisely that, Holmes," I averred.

"But, where is the blood man? Look around you, there is not a drop to be seen."

"Nevertheless, Holmes, it appears most strongly to be the case."

"Very well, let us state what little we know and proceed from there. He met his death some three hours ago, his body apparently drained of blood. We can rule out his being in the sea, so the question is, how came he here and perhaps more so, why?"

"Perhaps," I ventured, "he was intending to take an early morning swim and was murderously attacked before he could do so."

"And the murderer then calmly drains the body of blood by whatever means that may be, without leaving scarcely a drop to redden the sand and then makes off with the clothes of our would be swimmer, as none are in evidence. I think not, Watson."

"What can you offer in its place, Holmes?"

"Alas my friend, very little," Holmes replied.

"Could it be that he was murdered elsewhere and the body brought to this spot?" Jacobs put in.

"It would be a most curious thing for the killer to do, risking the chance of being seen. I see other insurmountable difficulties too and yet that must surely be how it happened."

"What are the difficulties, Holmes?" I asked.

"Firstly, gentlemen." he said, addressing the policemen present, "I noticed yesterday evening, that the sand is raked at the end of the day to ensure a smooth surface to start the day with."

"Yes sir that is the custom here," Sergeant Quick replied.

"Now, pray tell me, who has been in attendance on this grim scene this morning?"

"Ourselves of course, you three gentlemen, the gent who found the body and that's it, sir as far as I am aware."

"And I fear we must include our friend here," he said, pointing to the corpse. "Now the problems we have must surely present themselves to you; we can identify the footmarks made by the regulation police boots of our friends of the constabulary here, also those of myself, Watson and Jacobs. There is a further line of footprints here too, almost obliterated, but partnered by clearly defined paw prints, so they belong to our dog walker, but I cannot see any other prints at all and there are certainly no signs of the sand being disturbed as it would be if our friend here had been dragged in some manner to this spot."

"Could not all our prints have disturbed those of the killer and his victim?" I asked Holmes.

"I fear it would be an impossibility, some prints would surely remain."

"But if he was not in the sea and was neither carried nor dragged to this spot, nor walked here himself then I cannot see for the life of me how he came to be here, it's frankly impossible."

"You know my methods, Watson," Holmes said. "When you have eliminated the impossible, whatever remains, however improbable, must be the truth." he looked heavenwards as he said these words.

"Oh no! From the air? That is too fantastical for words, how can you possibly explain it?"

"I must confess I cannot do so at the present time, yet it must be so because it can be no other way. Notice how the body sits *in* the sand, not on, gentlemen, *in*, indicating an extreme downward pressure, surely then it is obvious that the body found its way here from the air."

"Are you suggesting that the body was dropped from a balloon or one of these new dirigibles, Mr. Holmes?" Jacobs asked.

"I suggest nothing, I only present what I know must be so, the body came from above," Holmes pronounced.

I was doing my best to take this in, it still seemed too fantastical for words and perhaps Holmes was guilty of looking for an ingenious, complex solution when matters were somewhat simpler. Just then, the sergeant and constable stood smartly to attention as the inspector arrived, introductions were effected all round. The inspector was a slight man, with pinched facial features as though he were permanently sucking on a boiled sweet. His clothes were ill-matched; I uncharitably thought he had perhaps dressed in the dark.

"Well, well, Mr. Sherlock Holmes on my patch......well, well," Baddeley said, and not, it has to be said, in a friendly way.

Sergeant Quick jumped in, "Mr. Holmes has some interesting theories regarding this matter sir."

"Amateurs like Sherlock Holmes always have theories, indeed, that's all they have, but it's left to the likes of us do to all the real work, we collect the evidence yet they take the glory." he said with a look of real contempt on his face. "There is no need of fancy theories here; no doubt a mad dog was responsible for the gaping wound I can see on this gentleman's neck."

"Inspector Baddeley, your conversation is most entertaining, but I do have certain matters pressing on me and regret I must leave your most interesting presence, all the better I am sure you will agree, to allow you to concentrate on doing all the real work. I bid you good day," Holmes said derisively.

I had come across policemen like Baddeley before, who were ignorant of the help Holmes had offered to police forces across the country. There were many, many cases where Holmes's name had not figured at all and the glory belonged to the police. Holmes often played the game for its own sake. I was heartily indignant on my friend's behalf although Holmes just laughed it off as being of no matter. As we walked away Holmes suddenly dashed off in the direction of the harbour wall closest to us. We followed in pursuit.

"We have something here doctors. Do you see this line of footprints?" Holmes asked, pointing at the sand.

We could indeed; a line of footprints which stretched quite clearly from the direction of the Cobb hamlet to the harbour wall.

"What do you make of them, Holmes, have they any bearing on this tragedy?" I inquired.

"Most assuredly so, Watson, but tell me, what do *you* make of them?"

"Well, the prints seem to go nowhere near our man, merely to the wall and then back towards Cobb hamlet," I opined.

"Yes, Watson, that is precisely what they do," Holmes said rubbing his hands together, almost triumphantly. "But look closer, my friend, tell me what you observe about them."

I always felt somewhat lacking when trying to apply Holmes's own methods, but I scrutinised the prints closely, I turned my eyes towards Holmes.

"Yes, Watson?"

"The footprints taking our stranger here to the wall are heavily indented as opposed to his return steps."

"Excellent, you scintillate today and what do you deduce from that?"

"Maybe he was running, Holmes?" I opined.

"Surely not, for the return steps clearly show an unchanged pace, the length of stride would lengthen considerably if he were running."

"Then what was he doing, Holmes?" I asked, with a touch of impatience in my voice.

"Simple, my boy, he was carrying a weighty load, but returned without it," he said. "You may be aware that I am familiar with the soles of sixty three shoes of British manufacture and this does not appear to correspond with any one of them, but has marked similarities to those produced in Eastern Europe although admittedly I am upon somewhat shaky ground there."

"The Count then?" asked Jacobs.

"I believe so," was the simple reply.

"There is a Russian ship in the harbour at the moment; the prints could belong to a member of the crew," I suggested.

"I think not," Holmes said. "The prints indicate shoes of the finest quality, not those you would normally associate with a humble crew member."

"And the weighty load you mentioned?"

"None other than our poor unfortunate friend on the beach, Watson."

"Good heavens! He is fully twenty-five yards from the wall here, are you suggesting the Count threw him?" I asked incredulously.

"Yes, I am suggesting precisely that my dear fellow."

"That is too much, Holmes, it is simply preposterous," I rejoined, "it would require superhuman strength, there must be another explanation."

"If you should chance upon another explanation, please be kind enough to bring it to my attention." Holmes promptly walked away, ignoring my objections. After he had gone a few yards, he returned with a strange expression on his face.

"Doctors, have you come to any conclusions concerning the nature of the wound?"

Jacobs was swift to answer, "Unfortunately, this may not correspond to the theory of murder you appear to be proposing, but I believe the wound to have been made by an animal of some kind, just as the inspector suggested. The lacerations and tears in the flesh suggest something like a dog to me, the incisions made by the canine teeth are quite prominent, yet the complete absence of blood is admittedly a barrier that I cannot rightly overcome."

"A dog, you say? Most suggestive. Capital," he said, rubbing his hands together again, turning his head to me, he said, "Watson, I fear I must leave you to your own devices today, I will spend some time in the excellent library at Exeter. By the way, did you bring your revolver with you on this trip?"

"Yes I did, force of habit I suppose," I admitted.

"Excellent. An Eley No. 2 can be a very persuasive argument indeed in a tight corner."

"What do you want me to do, shall I report your findings to the inspector?"

"I think not, his attitude was far too cavalier with me and I will follow my own methods here and will tell as little or as much as I choose."

"But what do we do about the Count? Would it not be the best course to interview him without delay and ascertain what he knows about this sad affair?"

"I have a strange notion that he would not be available for an interview along the lines you mention," Holmes replied.

"Then, once more, what can we do?"

"Nothing my friend, all we have is supposition and a seemingly queer theory, we cannot move without proofs, Watson."

"But I must be able to do something, Holmes?" I persevered.

"Nothing my boy, enjoy your holiday." And with that he was gone.

"What an extraordinary fellow your Mr.Holmes is," Jacobs exclaimed. "But, tell me, what do you make of all this?"

I admitted to Jacobs I was mystified, there was something diabolical happening here yet I could not even begin to conceive what it may be and the more I tried to reason the more bewildered I became. My thoughts were disturbed by Constable Street who had caught up with us. "Glad I caught you, Dr. Jacobs," he said breathlessly, "Dr. Pomphlett's boy, Percy was looking for you, the doctor is indisposed and there is illness once again in Silver Lodge."

"Silver Lodge? Where that poor girl Rose Hannington lived?" I asked.

"Yes, Dr. Watson, now her cousin Elizabeth is also taken ill."

"Tell Pomphlett's boy to run back and tell the doctor I will attend in his stead," said Jacobs to the constable.

"Very good sir, thank you. And, Dr. Watson, I apologise for the rudeness of my superior, Quick and me would be only too glad of your friend's help."

"Thank you, Street, I will inform Holmes on his return."

"Watson, will you accompany me to Silver Lodge? If Elizabeth should be suffering the same affliction that struck her cousin down then I would be only too glad to have your assistance and experience, I fear time may not be on our side."

"Of course, my dear fellow, I am at your disposal," I unhesitatingly answered.

"Thank you, Watson, I knew I could rely on you my old friend."

CHAPTER NINE

There was no time to procure transport for ourselves so we set off for the Hannington's at a brisk pace. Silver Lodge was just over a mile out of Lyme and our course took us up Haye Lane. I stole glances towards the Manor as I passed and I told Jacobs of the ugly confrontation I had suffered there. It was all quiet there today however, although I could not help, but steal backward glances at it. By the time we reached the top of the incline and turned towards Axminster we were both wheezing like old men. I reminded Jacobs that the last time we took any physical exercise together was on the occasion of our last match together for Blackheath. It was fully twenty five years ago and we both contributed points very late on to snatch a victory over our fiercest rivals, Richmond. We were both chaired off the pitch at the end of the match, a memory I will never forget and always treasure.

There was a narrow lane to our right, one hundred yards or so past the Black Dog Inn. I could see a house standing alone in extensive grounds, built on three floors out of a grey stone with glorious views across the valley and from thence out to sea. The decorative panelled door was opened before we had a chance to knock, by the lady of the house, Mrs. Irene Hannington, evidently awaiting our arrival most anxiously. We expressed our condolences at her recent sad loss and she accepted both them and us graciously.

"Mrs. Hannington," said Jacobs, who earlier had told me he knew the lady in question from various social functions they had both attended, "may I introduce Dr. Watson, an old friend and esteemed colleague? He is holidaying in Lyme for a few days and I hope you will forgive the liberty in my bringing him along, but I was of the mind that a second opinion may prove useful."

"Yes, of course, Dr. Watson is more than welcome, let me show you straight to Elizabeth's room," Mrs. Hannington replied.

"Before you do so may I just ask, Elizabeth is your niece, I believe I am correct in saying Mrs. Hannington?" I asked.

"Yes, she is my sister's child....both my sister and her husband were carried off during an influenza outbreak just two years ago, Elizabeth was just fourteen," Mrs. Hannington explained. "Rose and Elizabeth were so very close in every way. In spite of the two year age difference, people would very often mistake them for twins, such was the strong resemblance between them."

"Do you have any idea as to where or how your daughter and Elizabeth may have contracted this disease?"

"I think, Doctor, that perhaps you are in more of a position to answer that than I."

"Had they perhaps holidayed together recently or spent some time away from their familiar surroundings, were they prone to visiting the harbour for instance?"

"No, I schooled them myself here," She stifled a sob at this point with her use of the past tense. Having composed herself, she continued, "the only other place they went together is Haye Manor. Sir Peter Rattenbury, who owns the house, approached me and asked if the girls would like to assist in the cataloguing of the books in his extensive library. I was glad for them to do so as it would so clearly further their education. The house is now temporarily occupied by a visiting nobleman, a friend of Sir Peter's it appears. The girls did not care for a servant he employs and their visits ceased."

"Thank you, Mrs. Hannington, we will see Elizabeth now."

"Thank you, Doctor, this way please."

We climbed the highly polished stairs to the third floor; the whole house had that marked silence that I had always been aware of in a home that had lost a loved one. Fancifully, I once expressed it as the house being in mourning too. We were shown into a spacious bedroom, furnished lavishly. The French windows caught the eye, running from the ceiling to the floor with a small balcony outside of them, all the better to enjoy the wondrous vista.

Elizabeth Hill, Rose's cousin was sleeping peacefully albeit with somewhat laboured breathing. She was on her back with her head perfectly in the centre of the pillow, her long, dark hair splayed out framing her face. She had a ghostly pallor and I thought for one dreadful moment that she had already left us. In spite of her illness and emaciated condition she had a serenity about her that was hard to quantify, an inner peace which extended itself to her features.

"How long has she been like this?" I asked.

"For three days, Doctor," said Mrs. Hannington.

I found it hard to believe that having so recently lost her own daughter, Mrs. Hannington had delayed thus in calling for help, but the lady herself interrupted my thoughts.

"Dr. Pomphlett was sent for on that first day, Dr. Watson, but he could see no connection between the illness which carried away my daughter and that of Elizabeth here. He was of the opinion that Elizabeth's symptoms were the outwards signs of grief and that they would pass in time." Here, she stopped for a moment to once again compose herself, "My grief will never pass, gentlemen."

I took her hands and ushered her into the chair by the French windows, "I am no stranger to grief myself and I fervently hope all the happy memories you possess will sustain you through the dark times ahead." I returned my attention to Jacobs who had been examining Elizabeth closely. "There appears to be no sign of haemorrhaging, yet she clearly exhibits all the symptoms of blood loss," he said, "dysponea is present also, as is atrophic glossitis."

"A virulent disease of the red blood cells perhaps?"

"Perhaps, she certainly needs to take in iron, I have tablets with me to ensure she does just that," Jacobs said, "and I am giving some thought to transfusing her."

"Transfusing of blood is not something I have entire confidence in, the success rate is very variable indeed. Besides, would you have the necessary equipment to enable such an operation to take place?"

"Yes, I am confident I could do it, but as you say, it is a very hit-and-miss affair unless we maybe use a saline solution as a substitute."

"That is one option certainly. I would be happier with the saline as opposed to blood itself; I feel more research needs to be made into just why so many transfusions fail," I said, adding, "do you think removal to hospital may perhaps be our best course?"

"The nearest hospital is in Exeter and I fear the journey would be too much for her. We will administer the iron and make her as comfortable as we possibly can."

Elizabeth's breathing, so shallow just a few minutes ago, was now sounding a little more normal, a spot of colour was returning to her cheeks and I prayed that recovery was imminent. Whilst Jacobs attended to the intake of iron for the poor girl, I walked over to Mrs. Hannington who was gazing out of the window, deep in thought.

"Can she be saved?" was her earnest entreaty.

"I believe so. Tell me, Mrs. Hannington, has she eaten these past few days?"

"Not a morsel, Doctor, even in her waking moments she refuses food."

"Has she been suffering with extremes of heat or cold at all?" I inquired.

"I rather think she suffers with heat at night because in the morning when I look in on her, the French windows are invariably open," said Mrs. Hannington, adding, "it's usually during the daytime when she is at her best, she wakes and talks almost as she did before this malady took hold."

"Now," said I, "you must excuse my next question as it will be unbearably painful for you, but do Elizabeth's symptoms follow the same course as those that afflicted Rose?"

"Yes." sobbed Mrs. Hannington. My heart went out to this lady, who had suffered so horrendously and I was determined that tragedy would not be allowed to strike twice here. At this juncture, the young lady herself opened her eyes and as though still in some strange dream cried out, "Do not let him have me for pity's sake." With this, she once again closed her eyes only for them to open again moments later. "Hello, Aunty," she said weakly, "I am so sorry to be such an awful trouble to you."

"Oh my darling, you are nothing of the kind. These gentlemen are doctors, now, see how lucky you are, not just one doctor, but two," Mrs. Hannington said.

"Elizabeth, I am Dr. Jacobs, can I persuade you to eat something, you may begin to feel much better when you have done so."

"I cannot, Doctor," She replied in a calm yet weak voice.

"Some liquid then?" implored my friend. She nodded in acquiescence and I poured a glass of water for her, which Jacobs administered to her along with the iron tablets. "Now then Elizabeth, doesn't that feel better?" he asked.

As she laid her head on the pillow once again, I noticed a small wound on the side of her neck which had been concealed by her hair. On closer examination, which Elizabeth resisted strongly, we could see the wound consisted of two small puncture marks just above the external jugular vein. "Elizabeth, do you know how you came to have this wound?" In response, she merely pulled up her nightdress to try and cover the marks.

"Mrs. Hannington, do you have a pet which may account for these marks on your niece's neck?" I asked.

"We have no pets at all, Dr. Watson, owing to my husband's asthma."

"Could one have been brought in by a visitor perhaps?"

"My niece has had no visitors, save for myself and Bawden my housekeeper. Although one young boy from the town has attempted to see her, he is a different class you understand and I do not welcome his attentions. I have sent him away on several occasions."

"Who is this boy, he may possibly have gained admittance without your knowledge perhaps?"

"He is a Nathaniel Heidler, his mother runs a guest house in Coombe Street in the old town."

"Yes, I am familiar with the Heidler's; in fact my friend and I are guests there. Thank you, Mrs. Hannington."

Jacobs said, "What are you thinking, Watson, that these wounds have caused an infection which mimics the symptoms of anaemia?"

"Precisely that, Jacobs, but how that squares with the apparent blood loss I do not know."

I addressed Mrs. Hannington once more, "Forgive me again, my dear lady, but was the self same mark also present on your daughter's neck?"

"I did fancy I saw something of the kind, Doctor, but I was sure I must have been mistaken because when I dressed my daughter prior to her funeral, there were no such marks present." She broke down completely at this point, her whole body wracked with heart rending sobs. I escorted this brave lady downstairs and rang for a servant. A grey haired lady appeared within moments. "Your mistress is feeling unwell, could please bring her a cup of tea to restore her nerves?" She turned and left the room and Mrs. Hannington called after her, "Thank you, Bawden." Then, turning to me, "Whatever must you think of me Doctor?"

"Mrs. Hannington, I can see you are a very brave lady, the way you have kept going is admirable in my eyes."

"Sad as it is, life goes on. My husband is away a great deal on business, more so recently and he deals with his grief in his own way. I, for my part keep the house going and immerse myself in everyday life, but when the night arrives and sleep won't come, then everything becomes black, as black as anything could be."

Mrs. Hannington had inadvertently stumbled on to the way of things for me after my sweet Mary had passed on. Day times had their allotted routines either working at my practice or writing up cases that Holmes and I had been involved in, but when darkness fell I was stricken with an all consuming grief and sadness and there were days when I held my own life in no esteem at all and pondered whether my own existence was of any great worth.

"If you like, Mrs. Hannington, I could prescribe you a sleeping draught, you may find it a great help," I offered.

"No, Dr. Watson," she said firmly, looking horrified at my suggestion. "No, if such a palliate means a deadening of the senses, then, no. My memories are all that are left to me, what are a few sleepless nights to me compared with these remembrances of my beautiful daughter?"

Jacobs appeared just then, addressing us both, he said, "Elizabeth is sleeping soundly now, she has a little more colour and I am most hopeful regarding her recovery."

"Oh, that is wonderful news, Dr. Jacobs, thank you so much, please would you be good enough to call tomorrow?" Mrs. Hannington asked.

"Rightly, it should be Dr. Pomphlett who should be attending, but as he is indisposed I will certainly call in the morning and if you should have need before that time, please do not hesitate to send for me," Jacobs answered.

"Thank you, I am most grateful and, Dr. Watson, will you be able to break off from your holiday once more and attend too?"

"Yes, Mrs. Hannington, it would be my pleasure to do so. If you will excuse us, we will see ourselves out," I answered.

"What I fail to understand is where these marks could have come from, especially to be present on both girls, do you have ideas?" I asked as we walked along the path.

"I must confess I am in the dark also. I am acquainted with Sir Ernest Grattan, an expert in the treatment of blood disorders, who works in Exeter. I think our best course would be to wire him and ask for his assistance."

"An excellent idea. Does Dr. Pomphlett live close by? It may be pertinent to ask a few questions regarding Rose's illness; I would be intrigued as to whether our good doctor saw any marks upon her neck also."

"Yes he does, in fact we are only a matter of a few minutes walk from his house."

"Let us hope he is not too indisposed to see us then. Tell me my friend, would this few minutes walk be uphill at all?"

"Yes, how did you know?" he said, laughing.

I groaned inwardly and gritting my teeth, set off up another of those accursed hills!

CHAPTER TEN

Mercifully the walk was, but a short one to Dr. Pomphlett's. My whole body was in revolt against the exercise I was putting it through. My old wound was throbbing and my stomach was demanding to have its needs met, for I had rushed out this morning from Mrs. Heidler's without either food or any form of liquid refreshment.

Jacobs asked as we approached Pomphlett's house, "Have you any idea why Holmes should have taken himself off to the library at Exeter?"

"None whatsoever," I replied. "He did say, however, that the events here had put him in mind of a similar happening elsewhere, it may be he has gone to investigate that further. The events of this morning have certainly prompted his action I believe, but I can assure you Jacobs he keeps things hidden just as much from me as from anyone!"

"And do you think he really believes that this Count threw a fully grown man twenty five yards off the wall?"

"Incredible as it may appear, he does," I answered, "and once again, I feel that this too harkens back to the events that he now recalls."

Dr. Pomphlett's boy answered our rattle on the door and let us in. We could hear the doctor long before we saw him. "Who the devil is that, Percy ?.....the last thing I want is visitors....I am in no fit state to see anyone....send them away Percy..........send them away !!"

"Hullo, Pomphlett," said Jacobs cheerily as we entered the room, "how are you, old man?"

"Oh it's you, Jacobs.....as you can see for yourself, not very well, not very well at all," he answered with the glummest of expressions on his face.

He presented quite a sorry sight indeed, clad in a long nightgown pulled up to his bony knees with his feet sitting in a bucket of hot water. He held a compress to his head which gave off a very strong smell of laudanum.

"Physician heal thyself indeed!" he complained bitterly.

Jacobs introduced me and before we settled on our business here, I asked the doctor if Percy, his boy, could perhaps brew some tea for us. "Tea? tea?" he cried, "do you think I have provisions enough to feed all and sundry that may care to visit me?"

"I am sorry Doctor to put you to any trouble, but we have both been out since early this morning and as yet have been unable to partake of any refreshment, so you see, it would be a great kindness on your part to accommodate us," I implored.

"Yes, yes, very well." Raising his voice, he shouted, "Percy, Percy......could you brew some tea for our visitors......not too strong mind, not too strong!"

That having been done, I stated our business with the good doctor. "We have just come from the bedside of Miss Elizabeth Hill, who is gravely ill; you have seen her recently have you not, Doctor?" I asked.

Pomphlett replied in the affirmative.

Jacobs asked, "When first you attended Miss Hill three days ago, did you not consider that her illness was the same which had struck her cousin down?"

"It appeared to me that Miss Hill was suffering an extreme reaction to her grief and no more than that," Pomphlett replied, spluttering and coughing all the while.

"Did you not even admit the possibility?" I asked.

"No, sir, I did not, is my professional judgement being questioned?" he said testily.

I was quick to pacify him, "No my dear fellow, not at all, we are only here in the interests of Miss Hill and hopefully the three of us can aid her recovery together by pooling our resources and knowledge."

"Yes, of course, the recovery of the young lady is all important, please forgive my testiness, it is the indisposition taking over my senses you know."

"When you examined Elizabeth did you notice any marks or wounds on her neck in the region of the jugular vein, Doctor?" I inquired.

"I saw no such marks, although........"

"Yes, Pomphlett?" prompted Jacobs.

"Rose did have marks such as you have described, I could not ascertain exactly what they were or how she came by them, but also I could not rightly see what part they had to play in her disorder."

"As to that, Pomphlett, we are in the dark also. We have administered iron to the poor girl and she seems to have responded favourably," Jacobs said.

"Miss Hannington also responded to iron and vitamins, but overnight her energy was sapped anew. The pattern was the same for each day and each night. I was completely at a loss as to what to do, gentlemen," he said becoming agitated. "I did the best I could."

"Calm yourself, Doctor," I said, "no blame is being laid at your door."

The interview ended abruptly with a prolonged coughing fit from Pomphlett so we bade him good day. Jacobs was now running a little late for his surgery so our brisk pace of earlier became somewhat brisker. We were almost halfway back down Haye Lane before I realised that Percy, the confounded boy, had not delivered our tea!

I repaired to Mrs. Heidler's in order to have a much needed shave. I felt positively unclean in my present state. The door was open so I dashed straight upstairs to try and render myself how a gentleman should look. Having achieved this objective, I came down those rickety stairs in search of refreshment. Mrs. Heidler was in the scullery, surrounded by laundry which was in the process of drying. "Good morning Mrs. Heidler, you will have to forgive Holmes and me for rushing off this morning, no doubt you are questioning your decision to take in two demented souls such as us who keep such irregular hours."

"No, not at all," she laughed. "Would you like something to eat, Dr. Watson or have you managed to do so?"

"I have no wish to put you to any trouble, tea would suffice," I answered.

"It is no trouble at all, Doctor I assure you, sit yourself down in the parlour and read the newspaper. I will prepare a breakfast for you. Is Mr. Holmes with you?"

"No, there is no telling when he will favour us with his presence," said I.

"Very well, breakfast for one it is."

I found it difficult to concentrate on the newspaper; the recent events in Lyme Regis kept me fully occupied. No hypothesis I could come up with would explain all that had occurred. The mystery was certainly deep unless we were looking for connections and junctions where there were none. My thoughts were still wandering hither and thither when Mrs. Heidler appeared with yet another sumptuous breakfast. "Thank you, it looks splendid," I said.

"There is plenty of tea in the pot and more should you require it."

"Pray, bring another cup then and share it with me," I entreated.

"I hardly like to, Doctor, after all you are my guest here, it would be most familiar of me to sit at your table with you."

"My dear lady, we have just spent a most pleasant evening dancing together so please I insist, the laundry can take care of itself in your absence."

She gave in to my entreaties and having selected a cup from the dresser, she sat next to me at the table. She explained that she had heard about the body discovered on the beach earlier and wanted to know whether it was that which had taken Holmes and me out so prematurely this morning. I explained the circumstances surrounding the discovery, being careful to leave out one or two of the more salacious facts, in addition to omitting Holmes's rather outlandish, yet undeniably intriguing theory regarding Orlana. I recounted further our subsequent visit to Silver Lodge and the strange illness of Elizabeth Hill.

"Yes, poor girl, "she replied, "Nathaniel is exceedingly fond of her, yet is given short shrift by Mrs. Hannington when he has attempted to see Elizabeth. He is so worried she will fall a victim like her cousin Rose that he seems barely able to function and has become silent and withdrawn."

"Yes, Mrs. Hannington mentioned Nathaniel's visits. She may come round in time, Mrs. Heidler. She struck me as a fair minded woman who is merely being protective of her kin."

"You are no doubt right, but I truly wish her attitude would soften."

I asked her about her late husband and she talked at length, quite freely of him. They had met when she was but one and twenty and had fallen in love almost instantly. Fate had decreed that they were to spend only a few short, happy months together before Henry's tragic, but heroic death.

"Have you not considered marrying again at any time during these last fifteen years?" I asked, hoping the question was not too indelicate.

"I have put all my efforts into bringing up Nathaniel. And I doubted that the love I felt for Henry could ever be channelled toward another man."

"I am familiar with that feeling, perhaps a love like that only comes around once, or perhaps some are fortunate enough to know such love twice in their lives."

"I have not tested the water of that theory, you may be right; all the same I do get lonely at times."

"That is perfectly understandable my dear lady," said I, "but you may still meet someone who will inspire love in you. Nathaniel will shortly be a fine young man and will be pursuing his own life, what then for you?" I ventured.

"I believe in destiny, Dr. Watson, if I am to meet someone and fall in love with them then it will happen regardless of what I may do or where I may go."

"I am a great believer in destiny myself," I exclaimed. "I instinctively know when things are right and my feelings invariably guide me correctly."

There was silence in the room save for the ticking of the grandfather clock in the hall. It was keeping time with the beating of my heart which I felt, she must surely hear too. I was on the verge of saying more when she said she must return to her laundry and thanked me for a most pleasant interlude. I sighed as she disappeared back to the scullery. I could not be sure my feelings were guiding me correctly in this particular matter and yet I could not disguise to myself what I was beginning to feel for this lady.

She popped her head around the door at this juncture in my thoughts. "Dr. Watson?"

"Yes, Mrs.Heidler?"

"I was just, well, thinking, I would much prefer it if you were to call me Beatrice," she said.

"My pleasure....er.....Beatrice.....and please call me John."

"Thank you.......er......John," she said, laughing.

CHAPTER ELEVEN

I had no idea whatsoever as to when Holmes would decide to return from his errand so I was determined to put these mysterious events out of my mind as much as I could and enjoy the afternoon. It was once again a warm Spring day, perhaps the sun always shone here I mused, it certainly seemed that way to me.

I regretfully said goodbye to Beatrice and once more stepped out into the narrow confines of Coombe Street. I turned to my left which would take me towards the sea, but opted firstly to pay a visit to the church which occupied a lofty position on the eastern edge of the town. The architecture was a heady mix of Norman, medieval and later restoration, but the whole was most pleasing and I passed a full thirty minutes in there in complete admiration.

I walked out of the church and from there took a path to the side which led into the small cemetery. Immediately facing me was a gravestone. Busily tidying up the ground around it and adding fresh flowers was a young girl of no more than twelve years old.

"Hullo, young lady, you are doing a fine job there," I said.

"Thank you, I take special care of this one," she adjoined.

I thought it would appear insensitive to inquire whether it was a resting place of a loved one. The girl, sensing my quandary, spoke up again, "Mary Anning is buried here."

"Oh yes," I felt surer of my ground now, knowing the name from the history book I had read. "She collected fossils did she not?"

"Not *just* collected them, no," the girl said reproachfully, "she studied them too and discovered lots of wonderful things."

Under the stare of this girl's big, brown eyes, I felt suitably abashed.

"She is the most famous woman in Lyme......ever!" she added and continued, "one day I want to be as famous as her."

"I am sure you will be, young lady," I averred.

Just then I heard a disembodied voice shouting.

"Lydia.........Lydia."

"Is that you, are you Lydia?" I asked.

"Yes, it's my mother calling me......bye."

"Goodbye, Lydia," I called after her.

How refreshing to have come across that oasis of normality when all around seemed anything, but normal. I wandered through the cemetery, observing the graves, the faded letters on the gravestones making them very difficult to decipher, but they were all a part of Lyme's rich and varied past. Without really noticing, I had come all the way through the small cemetery to be met with yet another magnificent view. The whole sweep of the bay lay before me in all its glory. Although I am very much at home in the midst of a sprawling metropolis such as London, I decided I could very easily be persuaded to live next to the sea. Doctor Johnson had remarked 'to be tired of London is to be tired of life'. I think had he ever had the occasion to visit Lyme Regis, his sentiments may have been slightly different. Gazing on this sumptuous view, I could well understand how impossible it would be to ever want to leave it. Perhaps that may explain the many stories of ghosts and revenants abroad in this town. Although their mortal remains have crumbled to dust, they are still reluctant to leave this scene. I shook my head and reprimanded myself strongly for thinking such bizarre and fanciful thoughts.

I sauntered along the seafront; there was now the kind of activity that one associates with resorts such as this. All traces of the violence inflicted on that poor soul on the beach had been obliterated completely; indeed, looking at the happiness displayed all around me, I found it very hard to believe it had happened at all. Up ahead by the Cobb, I could see the imposing figure of Constable Street conversing animatedly with a few fishermen.

"Hullo, Street…..how goes the investigation?" I asked.

"Dr. Watson, well, it goes slowly sir although the inspector is sticking with the mad dog theory," Street replied.

"Did the mad dog then dress itself in the dead man's clothes?" I asked, laughing.

"Quite sir, Quick and me have said as much to the inspector, but being how he thinks we have not one brain between us, he pays us no heed," said he glumly.

"More fool he then, Street."

"Thank you, Doctor and in the meantime we have some good news of a sort. We have identified the body, well, not completely sir, but we have made a start towards doing so. I circulated a description of the unfortunate gent amongst the traders and fishermen who live and work around the harbour. Mr. Beviss who acts in the capacity of a supervisor at the bonded warehouse thinks he recognises him as the man who accompanied a foreign Count to pick up some boxes a few weeks back. Although the light was not good, he feels sure it was the same man."

"The Count again!" I exclaimed, before I could catch myself.

"Yes, Doctor. Inspector Baddeley has gone to Haye Manor where the Count is currently residing to see if he can shed any light on this morning's events." Street then looked at me strangely and asked, "Are you familiar with this Count then, Doctor, only you started so when I mentioned him?"

"No, no it was just that I have heard some such person mentioned once or twice since arriving here," I uttered weakly.

I have to say that Street did not look entirely convinced by my explanation and I soon excused myself and set off to stroll through the gardens above 'The Walk'. I have never been one to partake of alcohol during the day, I think those who know me best would consider me moderate in all things, but as the sun beat down upon me I had a sudden desire for another drop of that thirst quenching cider. It was, but a few minutes walk, all uphill of course, to the Volunteer Arms and the landlord was doing quite a roaring trade when I arrived there. I came across Sergeant Quick, who was huddled in the corner with some other men, playing cards. At his request I took my glass of cider over to their table and joined them.

"I was only telling these gentlemen a few minutes back that I had met the famous Sherlock Holmes this morning and blow me, in you walk, Dr. Watson," Quick declared.

At this they all laughed and I joined in the general merriment. One of them spoke up, "Where's he to then?"

"I'm sorry, "I said, "I didn't quite catch that."

"Where's......he.....to?" he repeated, as though talking to a slow child. I still looked puzzled so Sergeant Quick came to my rescue, "Where's Mr. Holmes now........off investigating?"

"Oh I see, I do apologise.....no, rather more mundane than that, he has gone to the library," I responded.

That news was greeted with more laughter, this time I resolutely refused to join in the mirth as I could not see what was remotely amusing about my friend visiting the library. I stayed only a few minutes more, making polite conversation, before making my way back to Mrs. Heidler's, to Beatrice's, I corrected myself in my head. On the way down Sherborne Lane I called in at Chapel Cottage to see Jacobs. He had just cut short his surgery for the day and was looking forward to a relaxing evening, especially so after his enforced early start. I told him that either with Holmes or without, I would see him later. I fully expected Holmes to be back very shortly however, not even he could spend that long in one library. Before I could make good my escape, Arthur and Cecil were upon me as one and in spite of my protestations to Mrs. Jacobs regarding the suitability of the tale, they would not let me go until I had regaled them with a condensed version of 'The Speckled Band'. I absolved myself of all culpability to Jacobs and his wife in the event that the children subsequently suffered from vivid nightmares.

I found a somewhat surprising guest at Mrs. Heidler's, none other than Inspector Baddeley. "Hullo, Dr. Watson, sorry to drop in on you like this, but I was hopeful of catching up with Mr. Holmes," he said.

"Why would you want to do that Inspector, I had the distinct impression that you rather disagreed with Holmes's way of doing things?"

"As Mr. Holmes was there at the beginning so to speak, I felt it churlish of me not to apprise him of the latest news, spirit of co-operation and all that."

His words did not impress me at all, indeed, I questioned his motive for being there at all, feeling sure he had come in order to try and score points off Holmes.

"And what, pray tell, is the latest news?" I asked.

"We now know that the gentleman in question was a servant or hired help of some kind to a Count Orlana, who is visiting these shores from Transylvania and is currently in residence at Haye Manor, the home of Sir Peter Rattenbury," Baddeley stated. "I have just come from there now."

I tried not to betray on my face that all this was already known to me, "And as for the murder itself Inspector, what news on that?"

"Murder!? There was no murder, Dr. Watson. It is my belief that amateurs like Mr. Holmes tend to look for outlandish crimes with which to test those outlandish theories they are prone to distilling to all us poor policemen, when very often the simple truth is overlooked."

" The simple truth here being?"

" The gentleman was attacked by a vicious dog after preparing to go for an early morning swim; that much was apparent to me this morning as I am sure you will recall," Baddeley replied. "There have been many reports of late concerning such a dog in the vicinity. That is where local knowledge comes in handy you see, otherwise we might all come up with any number of fancy theories."

"What do you suggest then, happened to the blood that would have been spilled, as there was none in evidence?"

"Oh, no doubt the tide would have washed it all away; there is no need to quibble over the small details anyway."

This provincial inspector was sitting there being absolutely insufferable and obviously had come here expressly for the purpose of scoring points off Holmes as I had surmised only moments earlier.

"How do you account for the footpr.."

My sentence was cut short by the strident voice of Sherlock Holmes; he was standing framed in the doorway, half out of his Inverness with a weighty volume of sorts under his arm.

"Inspector Baddeley, how good to see you. I believe I owe you an apology. I have been thinking about the matter all day and I have come to the conclusion that your mad dog theory really has a lot to recommend it. I really do feel that you have got to the heart of the matter."

Baddeley was rather taken aback by my friend's generosity of spirit. "Thank you Mr. Holmes, your apology is accepted. Well, gentlemen, I will bid you farewell, it has been a long, trying day."

"Inspector, Watson here will tell you that eavesdropping is just another one of my less desirable habits and I could not help, but hear you say you have paid a visit to Haye Manor to see Count Orlana."

"That is correct, Mr. Holmes, what of it?"

"I am not a betting man, Baddeley, I leave all such vices to my friend Watson, but I will wager the Count was not at home."

"I was informed by a surly, bad tempered fellow who evidently works there in some capacity that the Count was away on business and would not be back until nightfall, neither was this fellow of any help at all in shedding any light on the poor soul on the beach."

"Is it your intention to return to Haye Manor on the morrow?" Holmes asked.

"Yes it is, Mr. Holmes."

"Well," Holmes smiled, "I wish you good luck with that."

"Thank you, I fully expect to have this matter dealt with by noon tomorrow."

"Excellent," cried Holmes. "Well, Inspector, please do not let us detain you, as you rightly said, it has been a long and trying day for all of us. Goodbye."

Baddeley shot us both derogatory glances as he slunk towards the door, he was evidently not used to being dismissed so. Holmes sprang to the corner of the parlour, curled himself into the cosiest armchair available, drew up his knees and leaned forward, eyes shining.

"Are you now then, of the belief that no mischief was done this morning and events happened as Baddeley stated?" I asked Holmes.

"No, Watson, there was indeed mischief done as you have so eloquently put it. I merely concurred with the inspector so as to free ourselves of the shackles of the official force. I fear we must act alone from now on."

"Act? Act in doing what, Holmes?"

"Ah, Watson, all in good time," my friend replied. "I have had a most informative and enlightening day, one which has caused me a great deal of consternation too. My belief system has been shaken to the core as yours will be my friend, I can promise you that."

"You talk in riddles, can you not be straight for once?"

"Sorry, my good friend, I was thinking out loud more than anything, anyway I fear it must wait until later," Holmes answered.

"Have you spent all your day in the library then?"

"There and also a silversmith I sought out."

"A silversmith? Are we to have more riddles?"

"Apologies once again, I am only too aware of how much I try your patience sometimes, but Watson, tell me, do you trust my judgment?"

"Yes, you can have no doubts on that score surely."

"Excellent, now tell me about your day."

I filled Holmes in on all that had happened during the day, from the time that Street had caught up with Jacobs and me until the time I returned to Mrs. Heidler's. I had to stop and repeat myself many times as Holmes sought to clarify a point or two, he was particularly insistent that he had full details of Miss

Hill's illness, particularly with reference to the mark on her neck.

When I had at last finished my account, he perched on the edge of the chair and said appreciatively, "Watson, you fully justify my comments of yesterday when I opined that you habitually underestimate your own achievements, you have acquitted yourself wondrously well today. You asked all the relevant and pertinent questions. Excellent my boy, I could not have done better myself."

"Thank you, Holmes," I said, touched again.

"Is young Nathaniel at home do you know?"

"I do not know, shall I ask Beatrice, I mean Mrs. Heidler?"

"Yes, please do so," he said, arching his eyebrows.

Nathaniel was indeed there and entered the parlour at Holmes's bidding. Holmes was busy scribbling a note and when he had finished he asked if Nathaniel would deliver the note to Silver Lodge and place it into the hands of Mrs. Hannington.

"She doesn't really care for me, Mr. Holmes, perhaps you should send someone else, I really don't want to go."

"I understand that, Nathaniel, but when I tell you that this note will play a vital role in Miss Hill's recovery, you may want to reconsider." Turning to me, he said, "Watson, I must ask you to affix your name to the bottom of this missive, for, from your account of today's visit to Silver Lodge, you have earned the trust of this lady."

"Certainly," I said, taking the note from him and reading it through. "But what is all this Holmes? Holy Bible by the bedside........a crucifix of silver to be placed on your niece's neck.....a garland of garlic around the French windows.....or handles to be made secure with firm cord and another crucifix........your niece not to be left alone tonight............ Holmes, she will think me some kind of charlatan or worse."

Holmes ignored me and looked intently at Nathaniel, "Will you take it?" he asked the boy.

"Will it truly help Elizabeth, Mr. Holmes?"

"I certainly believe so, Nathaniel," Holmes replied.

"Then I have no choice, I must take it."

"Be sure to place it into Mrs. Hannington's hands, Nathaniel and implore her to follow the instructions in the note precisely."

"Trust me, Mr. Holmes," he said as he left the room.

"Holmes, can I now be told what the deuce is happening here, what was that cryptic note all about?"

"Not cryptic, assuredly not, the letter was plainly put and may well result in the saving of that poor girl's life, for there is an extreme evil at work here my old friend."

"I must confess it did not appear to be plain to me, rather more along the lines of mumbo-jumbo surely."

"I prefer to think of it as a statement of good and evil, but as I can smell a perfectly wonderful aroma from the kitchen, let us postpone further discussion on the matter until we have dined and then we will wander up to the good Dr. Jacob's house, where I will apprise you both on my findings."

It would have been no use whatsoever trying to browbeat Holmes further, once he had made his mind up that he was going to remain silent, no entreaties or petitions could ever sway him. Just then Beatrice came into the parlour. "Excuse me gentlemen, I need to lay the table for dinner," the fair lady said.

"May I give you a hand my dear?" I volunteered.

"Yes, that would be most welcome." She hesitated there and turned to Holmes. "Mr. Holmes, I could not help overhearing your remarks regarding this note that Nathaniel has taken at your request, you said there was an extreme evil at work."

"I believe that to be the case, I also believe it can be defeated," said Holmes.

"Have you put Nathaniel in danger? If any harm comes to him Mr. Holmes, I will hold you personally responsible and then you will truly know extreme evil, believe me. Tell me now, is he in danger?" she asked agitatedly.

"Mrs. Heidler, rest assured that your son is in no danger and his delivering of my urgent communication will, I hope, result in the saving of at least one life."

"Beatrice," said I, "I am sure Holmes meant no wrong in sending Nathaniel on this errand and I am equally sure he would like to apologise for his upsetting you by his actions." I looked pointedly at Holmes as I said this.

"Yes of course, I am sorry, Mrs. Heidler, forgive me. I certainly should have consulted you before sending your son to do my bidding."

To Holmes's credit, he managed to sound and look contrite during this exchange. I gave him a black look and went to the scullery in search of Beatrice. I found her sobbing pitifully, how my heart went out to her. I put my arm around her shoulders and motioned her to sit in the only available chair.

"Oh, John, "she cried, "what is happening here, whatever will I do if anything were to happen to Nathaniel? He is my whole life."

"Do not fear, nothing will happen to him, not only do you have Holmes's guarantee of that, but mine also. I will not allow any injury to come upon your son, that is my solemn promise to you, Beatrice."

"Thank you, John, you are such a kind and good man." At this, she kissed me on the cheek. "I am myself again now, come please give me a hand to carry the food in.

"It will be my pleasure, Beatrice," I said.

Holmes was still sitting in the armchair when we came through with the food. The volume he had under his arm was now lying across his legs and he was studying it intently with a strange look of horror on his face.

"Did you obtain that book from the library, Holmes?" I asked.

"Yes, as you can see I have added petty larceny to my motley collection of sins. Do not look so shocked my dear fellow; I will make full provision for its return in due course. I have memorised all the relevant details however."

"Then why pray, remove the volume from where it rightly belongs?"

"Because, my dear fellow, I wish you and Jacobs to see and read what I have seen and read, rather than just my recounting of its contents. Once you have done so, you will comprehend all the better what I believe we have to face and defeat here in Lyme Regis."

"More riddles, Holmes," I said reproachfully and instantly regretted doing so. "I am sorry my friend, I will be patient a little while longer."

The conversation during dinner once again veered away from any mention of the strange happenings and the presence of evil here, as Holmes had so defined it. It was one of Holmes's infuriating traits that he, whilst in the midst of a case, could detach himself almost completely from the problems that had been perplexing him and converse merrily about every subject under the sun. The subjects of our conversation that evening were as I recall, seventeenth century music, medieval Florence, Scottish malts and the Ottoman Empire. Holmes had the ability to discourse on these matters as though he had made some special study of all of them. Just as we finished eating, Nathaniel returned and informed us that in spite of the frosty reception Mrs. Hannington had afforded him, the note from Holmes bearing my name had been duly delivered to the lady in question. After she had studied it for a few moments, she told Nathaniel to tell me, all would be done as 'I' had requested.

"Excellent, thank you Nathaniel." Holmes then declared himself ready for the trip up to Chapel Cottage.

"But, Holmes you are still in your outdoor clothes as am I, I really think we should change before we go visiting."

"Good old Watson, ever the conventional one, very well, even at a time like this I suppose the conventions and rituals must be observed."

Fifteen minutes later, we bade Beatrice good evening and set off on the short journey to Jacobs's cottage. Holmes patted the volume he had borrowed from the library. "This may change your life, Watson and all that you hold dear," he said cryptically.

I shuddered involuntarily as though someone or something had walked over my grave.

CHAPTER TWELVE

A rthur and Cecil were still up when we arrived so yet again I was prevailed upon to relate a tale to them. At the suggestion of Holmes I treated them to an adventure that Holmes and I had in Devon a few years back. My account of this macabre tale has yet to be published, but it involved an escaped convict, an old curse, murder and a spectral hound. I have to say I did remonstrate with Holmes whether this tale was appropriate for younger children, but as I was out-voted by both Holmes, Mrs. Jacobs and the two boys, I had no recourse, but to narrate the story to them, being careful to play down the scarier aspects. It was a delight to see their animated faces as I told the tale. They got themselves very involved, hissing the villain and cheering Holmes and me with all the gusto they could manage. After another promise to tell them a further story on the occasion of my next visit, they finally succumbed to tiredness and went to bed happy, to a sleep which would hopefully be free of dreams about gigantic hounds.

Mrs. Jacobs had some finishing touches to apply to a watercolour painting she was working on so she excused herself and the three of us settled down in the sitting room with a glass of port and a cigar apiece.

"Gentlemen, I must beseech you to approach this evening with truly open minds, it is my belief there is evil at work here, an evil which falls outside of our hitherto known world, but one which I believe can be conquered," Holmes stated.

"Is the Count at the centre of things?" I asked.

"Yes, it is my considered belief that he is the embodiment of this evil I mentioned, Watson."

I shuddered at the sound of these words. I did not know as yet how Holmes had arrived at this conclusion, but in spite of my own doubts regarding the existence of a foe outside of the known world, I instinctively knew Holmes was right.

"You mentioned you had heard or read of similar events taking place elsewhere Holmes, was that the reason for your visit to the library?" I inquired.

"Yes, by the time we had assembled on the beach this morning to view that poor soul's remains, most of the account had come back to me and, indeed, the sad scene we encountered on the sand also harkened back to that account so struck from my memory. Firstly though gentlemen, I must tell you that during the night, whilst you, Watson were dancing to your heart's content, I stole out to the vicinity of Horn Bridge, hoping to encounter this so called spectre of Rose Hannington."

" And did you encounter this phantom, Mr. Holmes?" Jacobs asked.

"It was a long vigil, the tedium of which I alleviated by taking a good amount of exercise up and down Haye Lane. I saw no one initially, but in the early hours I saw a flash of white illuminated by the moonlight. It appeared to be flitting in and out of the trees that line the river. I crept closer, the better to observe. It was a young girl, gentlemen, of that there can be no doubt."

"And was she a girl of flesh and blood or.............?" my voice tailed away.

"She displayed all the vestiges of being so, Watson, yes."

"Perhaps then, she was indeed a real girl, maybe some one with a disease of the mind, who is prone to nocturnal ramblings," I opined.

"I fear not my friend, as I believe will become apparent. I followed her as best I could; once or twice she stopped and sniffed the air as though she could smell my presence. I stood absolutely still at those moments until the danger had passed. I followed her into a small spinney and I lost sight of her momentarily, but then I heard a scream through the trees, a fearful sound of an animal in its final death throes. I rushed through the trees and came into a clearing. In the moonlight, far in the distance I could make out a hint of white, the fleeing form of Rose. I committed myself to a search of the clearing. Were it were not for the moon shining so brightly I have no doubt I would have missed it, but there in the middle of the clearing was the body of a fox, its neck savagely exposed where the flesh had been ripped from it. The wound was bloodless, gentlemen and I have no doubt that were the body to be examined it would be found to have been exsanguinated. Admittedly, exsanguination did not come to my mind until the events of this morning."

"And Rose Hannington did this?" Jacobs asked incredulously, "is that what you are trying to tell us?"

"What once was Rose, yes."

"This is unbelievable," I exclaimed, "are you certain it was Rose or whatever she has become, that did this? And just what has she become?"

" Yes I am, Watson and for want of another expression, Rose has become one of the undead."

Jacobs was as perplexed as I, "Undead, Mr. Holmes…what on earth do you mean, undead?"

"Simply put, it is one who has died, but is unable to rest in peace," Holmes replied.

"Are you trying to tell us we are dealing with a ghost then?" Jacobs asked.

"No, it is not as simple as that. In bodily form the creature is Rose, hence young Selby recognising her, as did others that had known her in life. But her actions are not her own, she has no free will in what she has become and what she has to do, she is akin to an automaton."

"But how can she still be flesh and blood, to be able to attack and maim, she is dead and in her grave surely?" I asked.

"She is dead certainly, Watson, but most assuredly not in her grave, as you can see from her actions as I myself witnessed."

"To what end though, Holmes?" I asked.

"To perpetuate the unholy alliance she has joined against her will, the alliance of vampires who must seek out and devour fresh blood in order to render themselves immortal and also to remain in that state."

"Vampires?" said Jacobs. "What nonsense is this, Mr. Holmes? I don't understand a word of this and what is this talk of immortality? Surely only God and the heavenly angels are immortal?"

"Do you believe in God then, Doctor?"

"Why, yes, Mr. Holmes I do." Jacobs replied.

"So, you also believe in good or, more specifically, the power of good?"

"Yes, certainly"

"And the Devil, do you believe in him also?"

"As a concept only; the Devil stands for the human race's predisposition for cruelty, for its innate ability to kill, maim and corrupt."

"Why should the Devil be just a concept and not God?" Holmes asked him.

"It is a question of faith, Mr. Holmes."

"But, surely, Doctor, one cannot accept the existence of good without evil?"

"Evil things happen, of course they do, only a fool would deny it, but they are random acts committed by human beings, not perpetrated by what you choose to call the undead."

"I choose to call her undead because that is precisely what she is. Believe me, gentlemen before the next few days are out we will all have to be prepared to question some very fundamental truths that we may formally have held dear."

"Please forgive me, Mr. Holmes, but I must reserve my judgment on that. I am of the opinion that any evils abroad in Lyme at this present time are more to do with human villainy than any supernatural sort."

I put a question to Holmes, "Do you say then, that this Rose creature was responsible for the fatal attack on the beach?"

"The footprints we found would point another way I believe, firmly in the direction of the Count. Besides if my facts are correct, then the undead creature that was formerly Rose has not yet attained the enormous strength that these beings can possess," Holmes replied, "if you remember, Victor Selby was able to repel her attack, albeit with a struggle."

"How is it you know about these being's strength, Holmes?"

"All will be revealed in this volume, Watson," said he, tapping the book with his long bony fingers.

" Then, Orlana, too, is one of these blood devouring creatures, vampires I believe you called them just now, hence his own strength displayed in hurling that poor soul off the harbour wall."

"Yes, in fact I believe him to be what you might call a Lord among vampires, if that does not sound too fanciful."

"My dear Holmes, the whole thing is fanciful and grotesque," I laughed, although the laugh belied my growing fear.

Jacobs had gone quiet, deep in thought, so I put a further question to Holmes, "The episode that these events here put you in mind of, where did it take place? Did the occurrences there follow a similar pattern?"

"It happened in Norway some ten years ago. As you know my correspondence is extremely varied and I had a letter or two on the subject by a learned friend of mine on the continent. Originally I came across it in a journal of sorts and promptly forgot all about it, but yes things happened there as they have done here, a mysterious vessel arriving in the harbour, a stranger then appearing followed by outbreaks of an inexplicable illness, also a violent death. I found the journal in question in the excellent library in Exeter, but it gave me no more details than I have just given you, other than the rumours which abounded of a visitation by the Devil himself upon that quiet Norwegian fishing village."

"But why this talk of these vampire creatures?" I asked.

"Those were the views expressed by my friend. He had made a special study of these creatures and ignoramus that I am, they had completely shifted from my mind," he replied, "at the time I have to say, I was every bit as incredulous as you are now."

"Does the volume you have with you, that you require Jacobs and me to read, contain the journal then?"

"No, Watson, this is something different altogether, something you will not easily forget. This be your introduction to the vampire."

I knew not entirely at that time what that word meant, but I shuddered again.

He put the book on the dining table behind his chair and motioned us to join him there. He turned the tome towards us so we could see the title clearly;

'The Mythology and Folklore of Eastern Europe' (1891)
By Professor Trelawney West

"Do not worry gentlemen, you are not required to read all of it, let me turn the pages to the relevant section......ah yes.....here we are."

Transylvania:

Vampires Goblins and Spirits

The people of Transylvania as a whole are extremely superstitious and believe devoutly in all manner of spirits, elves and goblins. I found many customs which involved appeasing wicked spirits by means of sacrifice prevalent, even when such traditions have long died out in other parts of Eastern Europe.

In general, they would never approach a cemetery without first crossing themselves for it is believed that even in consecrated ground Evil Ones lurk ready to trap unsuspecting souls. Their most morbid fear is of the vampire, an undead, unclean malevolent being. The vampire is feared throughout the region as a collector of souls, this is easily accomplished by the drinking of blood which is a life preservative for the vampire. The victim falls prey to this evil without being aware of the fact, often when they sleep. The vampire sinks his very pronounced canine teeth into the victim's neck and drinks freely of the victim's blood. When seven days have elapsed, the poor unfortunate soul dies of an apparent wasting disease and in turn becomes one of these unclean creatures, the undead. His perverted taste is for young girls to become his so called brides.

The vampire is compelled to sleep during the day for bright sunlight will turn him back to the dust from whence he came. He rests in his coffin or in his native soil and becomes re-animated with nightfall when his blood lust compels him to seek out new victims. He has prodigious strength and the ability, it is said, to change shape at will, be it a dog a bat or another beast of the night. The vampire will employ mortal helpers, either under duress or with promise of reward, to ensure the vampire's resting place during the day goes undiscovered.

Although all the accounts I have uncovered describe the vampire as being immortal, there are ways listed in which to effect the destruction of this profane being. There were I found, localised differences, but the common ways noted were, the driving of a stake through the vampire's heart while he is at rest, the exposure to sunlight and a silver bullet fired directly into his heart.

As protection in the first instance from these parasites the locals would employ a crucifix, preferably fashioned from silver. Holy water was also used to ward off vampires as was a simple Bible. I heard many tell of garlic being employed around doors and windows to stop the creature gaining entry. I collated reports of these creatures throughout Eastern Europe, but they were of a sporadic nature. Nowhere was the fear so inbuilt in the people as it was in the region of Transylvania.

"There you have it, gentlemen, I believe that what you have read there perfectly reflects what has been occurring here," Holmes declared.

Even with all my trust in Holmes's judgment, I still had great difficulty in believing that one of these foul creatures was here in Lyme Regis and I could see Jacobs was grappling with the same problem. "Perhaps, Holmes," I ventured, "Count Orlana is masquerading as one of these vampires for some nefarious reason, or to perpetuate some occult group."

"No, Watson. I believe he is one of these creatures, to suggest otherwise ignores the evidence we have both seen and heard."

"Do I understand then, that Elizabeth was to be his next victim, his 'bride' as this book describes it, in the same way Rose is now his 'bride'?" I asked, still mystified.

"Yes, hence my scribbled note to Mrs. Hannington outlining all the precautions that were to be taken to ward off the Count"

Jacobs seemed reluctantly to be coming around to the view that maybe this vampire was indeed a reality, "But how, Mr. Holmes did he gain admittance to the bedroom of Elizabeth, or, indeed Rose for that matter? Elizabeth's bedroom is on the third floor with no nearby piping or ivy to assist an ascent to the balcony outside her window."

"The article we have just read mentioned his ability to change shape and I think the key lies in this. For instance, turning himself into a bat would certainly ensure an easy and novel passage to the balcony," Holmes replied matter of factly as though he were talking about the most commonplace of actions.

My mind was racing with a hundred and one questions….."Is it your belief that the Count arrived here on the schooner in spite of the protestations that he knew nothing about the shipping arrangements?"

"Yes, it seems the most likely happenstance. I assume the crew would have been despatched to their Maker in much the same way as our friend on the beach and then thrown overboard to a watery grave."

"The paragraphs we have just read implied the vampire goes about his murderous business slowly and surely over the course of seven days, why then the savagery meted out to the body on the sand?" I inquired.

"I think there we are in the realms of conjecture, Watson, but a servant who had possibly seen or heard too much, or had asked for more than the Count was willing to give him. It may be simply that he had outlived his usefulness or the Count's blood lust was at its apex."

"How then, in God's name are we to defeat this malignance?"

"By employing the methods we have learned about tonight, thanks to the diligence of Professor Trelawney West."

"But surely all of this is just folklore, Holmes, how can we be sure these methods work?" I asked.

"At the moment, Watson, it is all we have to work with."

"But we have no silver bullets, neither can we force the Count into daylight. That only leaves the stake through the heart and to do that we have to find his resting place, it seems an impossible task, particularly as we have no real idea that any of these methods will actually work."

"You forget my visit to the silversmith, Watson. Alas, my credit is not as good in Devon as it is in London, but I managed to come up with sufficient funds to enable a silver bullet to be fashioned which will sit admirably in the chamber of your service revolver, my old friend."

"And if we fail?" interjected Jacobs.

"We must not fail, gentlemen," Holmes said fervently.

"Can we not involve Inspector Baddeley and the official force in this Holmes?" I asked.

"I fear we would be locked up as madmen. No, we must act alone in this; involving officialdom would also mean the affair would become public knowledge with the resulting panic that would bring. Besides, my friends, I believe that we three are the best equipped to deal with this, with what we have gleaned from this volume this evening."

There was a desperate silence in the room, a silence which spoke volumes which grew as we all contemplated the dark deed we had set ourselves, what chance had we against an enemy such as he? Yet the article had clearly stated that these vampires, these abominable creatures though seemingly immortal, can be destroyed and destroyed they must have been in the past, otherwise what or who could possibly have stopped them from dominating the earth?

A loud knocking at the door brought us all back from our thoughts and yes, fears too.

"It is most probably a patient, as a rule they show scant regard to confining their visits to those hours when the surgery is officially open," said Jacobs.

Mrs. Jacobs called out that she would attend to it and send them away if the call proved to be not urgent. There followed a few moments of conversation in the hall, during which we could hear Sarah laughing and then she ushered the visitor in. A tall man, clad all in black with a gleaming bald head and eyes which bore straight into my very soul it seemed. Even before he spoke, we knew of course, who and what he was.

"Gentlemen, my name is Count Orlana," he said in a voice that chilled my very existence.

CHAPTER THIRTEEN

The air around the Count gave the impression it was in constant motion, swirling around him as though it were part of the man, rendering him almost ethereal. It was as though all the molecules in his body were busily re-assembling themselves because a few seconds later solidity seemed to return to him. For a long, long moment not a word was spoken by anyone, we were taking stock of him in much the same way as he was with us. That we were in the presence of evil was undeniable; it was a tangible thing which we all felt. Orlana's base self was readily apparent and I believe even without the foreknowledge we had acquired that evening, we would still have felt and recognised it. Turning to Mrs. Jacobs, he bowed extravagantly, "Thank you for the most cordial welcome into your household," as he said this in a measured accent less tone he lightly brushed her long hair away from her face so it revealed her neck briefly. He smiled lasciviously.

Both Jacobs and I sprung up from our chairs, Jacobs started for the Count, "Sir, I must ask you…….."

In the blink of an eye, Orlana had covered the yard or two between the two men, gazing straight into Jacob's eyes with peculiar, protuberant, staring eyes of his own. He said, "Do not alarm yourself Doctor, my needs are fulfilled………*for now.*"

Jacobs visibly blanched at these words and obviously greatly distressed, spoke a few kindly words to Sarah. She was reluctant to leave us with this out of the ordinary character, but she did so and we were left alone with the Count.

The Count had an expression on his face which was both triumphant and condescending, it seemed to say to me, 'I will win, do not tamper with me, you are just puny fools'. Once again, it led me to ponder how this evil creature could be defeated. As Holmes had done so many times in the past, so Orlana did now, cutting into my thoughts, "You are correct in what you are thinking, I cannot be defeated by the likes of you, you have no conception of what you are up against," he said directly to me, his words seemed to reach me in a cloud of icy vapour which emanated from his mouth.

"My name is Sherlock Holmes," my friend said, "the gentleman you have just addressed so expressively is Dr. Watson. Pray, take a seat, Count."

" Thank you, I prefer to remain standing," the Count retorted.

"As you wish," said Holmes.

We all settled back into our chairs and I, for one, was struck by the incongruity of the situation. We were observing the niceties of polite conversation with an inhuman beast, who according to Holmes and from what we had comprehended ourselves, was a being who killed mercilessly and claimed souls as his own, to do with as he wished.

Holmes spoke first, "What may we do for you, pray, tell us the purpose of your visit?"

"I have a simple request for you, Mr. Sherlock Holmes as I have already intimated to your friend Dr. Watson here, do not tamper further with my plans or obstruct me in any way at all."

"I am very much afraid that I can give you no such assurance, I am equally sure the same applies to my good friends here."

We gave our affirmations to Holmes and were the recipients of our visitor's malevolent gaze.

"Mr. Holmes," said the Count slowly, "it may surprise you to know that you are known to me. You are a meddler, but if you persist in this course, there can only be one outcome. I strongly urge you to reconsider."

"Our view of the outcome is of course, entirely different, I am sure you can see that."

"Tonight, already, you have interfered with my plans, thinking yourself so clever to have done so, but you may find it is the only victory allotted to you. I will not be crossed again. You know not who you deal with."

Holmes pointed towards the volume where it still lay on the table, "On the contrary, I believe we have a fairly good idea of who and what we deal with and the methods we can also employ against you."

"Mere fairy tales, Mr. Holmes, fairy tales. Do not believe that I can be stopped by the methods the peasants of my country would have you believe. Many men have tried their hands at my destruction through the centuries..........*and yet, as you see, I survive.*"

"Centuries?" I exclaimed incredulously.

"Yes, Dr. Watson, centuries! I was born into a noble family in a remote area of Transylvania in the year 1384."

"Are you asking me to believe that you are over five hundred years old? My eyes tell me otherwise."

"I tell you it is so. The blood I drink preserves me in the state you see now. So you see, I am truly immortal. Compared with myself and those of my kind you are detestable, you are nothing. Now tell me, would you not wish for eternal life for yourself, Doctor?" the Count asked of me.

Holmes responded for me before I had a chance to open my mouth, perhaps he feared my rashness would result in God knows what for me. "An eternal life of what? Spreading fear and misery? Of cowering in the shadows?"

"No, Mr. Holmes. A life of supreme power, of illimitable control. I have ranged across this continent seeing history being made, at times you might say, I have created some of that history as my empire has grown," he said expansively.

"And in five hundred years, just where has your empire stretched? To Dorsetshire. To a small town sited obscurely on the coast. Not much of an empire I am sure you agree, Count. And the power you speak of is not supreme. The control you think you possess is far from illimitable. You are bound by the laws of nature, the pure and natural daylight, the power of the sun, these things can destroy you," Holmes said, goading him dangerously I thought.

"More fairy tales that you choose to believe because the truth is too much for you to comprehend. It is how I have stated it, Mr. Holmes, only a blind, despairing fool would think otherwise."

"I obviously belong in that category then, Count," responded Holmes.

"Not for long I assure you. If you continue on your present course, your worthless existence will come to an end. Perhaps then and only then you will acknowledge my words are true."

"It may be so that my existence could be said to be worthless, indeed, I have often thought it myself, but believe me, Count, effecting your destruction will be the culmination of my efforts on this earth and I fancy that I can then retire, knowing that my life at last had some permanent worth."

"Retirement, Mr. Holmes will not be an option for you, your outspokenness has sealed your fate, your destruction at my hands will give me the greatest of pleasure. I promise you death, Mr. Holmes."

" I have been promised that particular state many times before, Count Orlana……….*and yet as you see, I survive*," Holmes said, flinging the Count's own words back at him.

The Count turned to Jacobs and me, "You have much to lose gentlemen, ask yourselves, do you really want to die in this way, a fool's death, on a fool's errand?"

"I think," said I, "for my part I would be glad to sacrifice my life in the pursuit of seeing the end of you and your foul, evil ways and if death should come my way, it would be that of a hero, not a fool."

"You are indeed a fool then," he hissed at me. "Dr. Jacobs, are you willing to consign your young family to a fatherless and husbandless existence?"

Jacobs was understandably angry. "Leave my family out of this," he shouted and before either of us could stop him, he charged headlong at the Count.

The Count shot out an arm and, barely touching my friend he sent him reeling across the room with terrific force. I rushed to his aid as he lay crumpled on the floor. He was badly shaken, but otherwise appeared unhurt.

"Well, Count, Dr. Jacobs has been exceedingly courteous in allowing you into his family home, but now I must ask you to leave, the good doctor prefers his guests to be those of the living variety," Holmes stated quite calmly.

"A final warning to you all, if you seek me out....it is I who will find you. I suggest you pray to your God, gentlemen, while you still can as your time is running out."

"Thank you for your most timely warning, unfortunately we cannot rightly see our way clear to heeding it, but I do have a warning for you also."

"Very well, Mr. Holmes, I will let you speak, it is the custom, is it not, for a condemned man to say a few last words."

"It is my desired aim and intent to destroy you and if that should involve damning your soul to eternal suffering in the fires of hell, then believe me, it will not weigh heavily upon my conscience. Goodnight."

The Count threw his head back and laughed, a demoniac laugh that echoed all around the room. "Until we meet again gentlemen," he swept his cloak around him and was gone.

Jacobs got to his feet somewhat unsteadily and sank into the chair. "My God, Mr. Holmes. What in the name of all that's sacred was that......that.....thing?"

" Precisely what we knew him to be, Dr. Jacobs."

"How can we defeat him, surely he holds all the advantages?"

"As much as the Count would have us believe that the methods of his destruction are no more than fairy tales, there was something which told me otherwise."

"What was that, Holmes?" I asked.

"Did you not see it in his eyes, gentlemen? Perhaps not, as most of his remarks were addressed directly to me, but unmistakably I saw in his eyes, fear."

"Fear? Surely not, Holmes. Why would such a creature fear us?"

"Because he believes that we could indeed be the agents of his annihilation," Holmes stated.

"Then why did he not simply do away with us here tonight? We had no weapons with which to fight him, he would have been free of us in moments."

"I think that even the Count has to be a little more circumspect than that, the undue attention our deaths would have caused may result in prompting others to find out what we have discovered about the true nature of our nocturnal friend."

"And yet," I said, "he did not appear to be quite so circumspect when he left that horribly mutilated body on the sand for all to find."

"Yes, I cannot wholly account for that, although it may have been some kind of warning."

"But, surely he intends to do away with us anyway," I said, shivering at the thought.

"Yes, Watson he does. We can have no doubts on that score. Perhaps, on his own terms, on his own territory, these are only surmises though."

"How do you intend to proceed, Holmes?"

"Firstly, I have to say my friends that the Count is correct when he says you both have much to lose. I have committed my life to combating evil in all the shapes and forms I have encountered it in, but I cannot reasonably expect you to join me in this venture when your lives, if not your very souls may be at stake."

"My old friend, I will not let you face this adversary alone. We have faced many dangers together and if this should be the final one, then so be it, but I will be by your side Holmes."

Holmes appeared greatly moved by these simple words of mine. "Thank you, Watson, thank you my dear friend," he said softly.

Jacobs rose to his feet and paced around the room agitatedly. "What consequences do you think will result if we should fail to end this creature's evil existence?" he asked.

"Almost certainly more deaths here until such time as he may decide to move on. It is fair to assume he will be on his travels at some time to spread his poison further."

"Then, Mr. Holmes, I will join forces with you, we have more chance surely of defeating him if we are three."

"Thank you, Dr. Jacobs, I know it would not have been an easy decision for you to make," Holmes said warmly, clasping him by the hand.

"The Three Musketeers," said I.

Two perplexed faces turned in my direction.

"All for one and one for all," I quoted

"Yes indeed, Watson," said Holmes.

CHAPTER FOURTEEN

In spite of our brave talk, the evening had ended on a sombre note when we all realised the enormity of the task we had set ourselves; this vampire, this creature had survived over five hundred years if he was to be believed and none of us saw any reason to doubt his words. There must have been countless attempts by God fearing people, acting on the side of righteousness to rid the world of this malignant growth, yet all must have failed and now it was our turn to destroy or be destroyed. What kind of a world would we be leaving behind if we failed?

I hardly touched the splendid breakfast Beatrice had prepared for us. I had promised Holmes not to speak to her of the things we had discussed and she must have been wondering what was wrong with me. I must have presented an abject sight to her eyes. I felt and no doubt looked as though I was in the midst of some horrible nightmare, a nightmare that even daylight failed to break the stranglehold of. Conversation between us was rather stilted. The chilling thought struck me that this might be the last breakfast we would ever share together. Holmes was going to accompany Jacobs and myself in our promised visit to Elizabeth Hill that morning. We had high hopes that the precautions we had taken to keep the Count away from her would result in a dramatic recovery in the girl. I voiced this.

"Are you confident, Holmes that the protection we attempted to afford the poor girl has worked?"

"Yes, my dear fellow, the proof was surely there in the unexpected visit of the Count. Having been denied access to Miss Hill, he sought out those who had foreseen and checked his plans."

"I hope to God you are right."

We finished our meal in silence, so much could have been said, but so much went unsaid. We made ourselves ready and we heard Jacobs rapping on the door shortly after nine o' clock. It was a warm, but overcast morning as we set out by the path which ran alongside the river. I was musing on the juxtaposition of the beauty I could see around me to the ugly, evil creature we had encountered yesterday evening. Perhaps in the same way that good has to co-exist with evil, beauty has to be balanced by ugliness. Every coin has two sides to it I concluded, not very originally it must be said.

After yet another ascent of one of Lyme's hills, we reached the top of Haye Lane and turned towards the track which would take us down to Silver Lodge.

"Is that Silver Lodge I can see there, Watson?" asked Holmes, pointing at the house in question.

"Yes it is."

"Is it possible to see young Elizabeth's room from here? "

"Yes, Holmes, it is on the third floor, the one with the French windows and balcony."

"Run!" shouted Holmes, "quickly now."

"What is it, Holmes?"

"Look, man, the French windows, they are open," Holmes cried wildly.

We ran after Holmes, but he was far too quick for us. I was full of foreboding as to what we would find and fervently hoped the explanation would be found to be innocent enough. When we reached the house, Holmes had gained admittance and was conversing animatedly with Mrs. Hannington. She looked up as I came in to the hall, tears in her eyes. "Dr. Watson, something dreadful has occurred....my niece is gone," she cried.

"Gone.....but, how?"

"You vouchsafed her safety to me, Doctor, you have failed me miserably."

"I am truly sorry, Mrs. Hannington; I would not have had this happen for the world."

"Apologies are not enough, Doctor, I want my niece back unharmed," she sobbed.

"Mrs. Hannington, the note which appeared to come from Dr. Watson came from myself, the good doctor only affixed his name to the note at my request, if anyone is to be blamed for this catastrophe, it is I."

"I did not understand your note I have to say, but went along with it and applied its contents diligently and now................" her voice tailed off as she broke down in tears.

"Are you able to tell me what has happened, Mrs. Hannington?" Holmes asked gently.

"I will try. Bawden my trusted housekeeper volunteered to sit up all night with Elizabeth. She assisted me in taking all the precautions you had listed in your baffling note. I insisted on being woken early to be sure in my own mind as to Elizabeth's safety and well being. Bawden duly came to wake me in accordance with my instructions. She reported that Elizabeth was sleeping soundly, her breathing was normal and her night had been extremely restful. I thanked Bawden and dismissed her so she could have a proper sleep herself."

"What time was this, Mrs. Hannington, please be accurate if you can?"

"It was early, I know that much, the sun had not yet risen."

"Thank you, and then?"

"I went back to sleep with a much sounder mind. I slept until shortly after eight. On waking, I went to Elizabeth's room to find the windows flung open and no trace of my niece. Oh my God, what has become of her?"

"What did you do after discovering her disappearance?" Holmes asked.

"I roused Bawden who was absolutely distraught. I have despatched her to fetch Sergeant Quick."

"Watson, Jacobs, could you stay with Mrs. Hannington while I examine Elizabeth's room?"

"Yes, of course, Elizabeth's room is the..........."

"Do not worry, I will find it," he called to me as he dashed away up the stairs.

Holmes had only been gone seconds when Bawden returned with both Sergeant Quick and Constable Street; she immediately went to her mistress's side.

"What brings you here then, Dr. Watson?" asked Quick.

"Watson is here with me, Quick, Mrs. Hannington asked us both to attend upon Elizabeth this morning." Jacobs said.

"I see, Dr. Jacobs. When did you last see her, Elizabeth that is?"

"Yesterday morning."

"And how was she?"

"Very ill indeed."

"This whole thing may be something of nothing, she may have woken and feeling better and decided to avail herself of some fresh air," Quick opined.

"I do not think that is very likely, Sergeant," I interjected, "this girl is gravely ill and a dramatic recovery such as you propose would be impossible."

"I bow to your superior medical knowledge, Doctor," he said superciliously.

Quick and Street asked Mrs. Hannington if they could see Elizabeth's room, when she nodded her agreement they invited Jacobs and me to accompany them. We trooped up the stairs. I was imagining the surprise on their faces when they encountered Sherlock Holmes there.

When we reached Elizabeth's room, Holmes was lying full length on the carpet by the French windows. He ignored our presence and carried on with a minute search of the room, examining every surface with his lens. Nothing ever seemed to escape his eagle-eyes, he was the most thorough man I had ever met.

At long last, he acknowledged our presence and that in particular of our visitors from the local police force.

"Good morning," he said, putting his lens away, "does the attendance of your good selves also indicate an impending visit from Inspector Baddeley?"

"Yes, "said Street, "he will be here very shortly as he stayed in town last night at the 'Sea View' boarding house."

"May I be so bold as to inquire what you are doing here sir?" asked Quick in an official tone.

"I merely accompanied the two doctors on their errand. I had a notion the exercise would be of great benefit to me."

"Is there anything that strikes you about this room that would in any way help account for the young lady's disappearance?" asked Street.

"Alas, very little. The room has furnished me with no clues."

"No clues, Mr. Holmes?" said the Inspector with mischief in his voice as he entered the room, "surely you have some theory or other to expound to us."

"Ah, Inspector Baddeley, I am pleased to see the earliness of the hour has not affected your repartee," Holmes declared.

Ignoring my friend's cutting yet apt remark, the Inspector applied himself to an examination of the room. He was done within a minute. "Really, Mr. Holmes, I thought you said the room furnished no clues, but you have missed the obvious one; the windows were opened from the inside. I would imagine by the girl herself, maybe to keep an assignation, who can tell with young girls these days?"

"Why would she have needed to open the windows then, there is no easy descent to the ground, surely she would leave by the front door," Holmes pointed out.

"It was a ruse, that's what it was, Mr. Detective, so we would all think of abduction before anything else; she does not want us to know she left of her own free will."

"I am most intrigued, Inspector. Pray, answer me this, what would have possessed the young girl to think that we would believe her to be abducted from the balcony, we are three floors up remember, with the attendant difficulty I have just described to you?" Holmes said, toying with the inspector.

"You are far too concerned with these small details, Mr. Holmes, my advice to you is to concentrate on the evidence you can see or, in your case, the evidence you have missed. Now, if you will excuse me, I must go and interview the lady of the house."

He swept out of the room with his officers in tow and descended the stairs.

"The man is insufferable, Holmes, why do you let him speak to you so?"

"It really is of little or no consequence to me my dear fellow, in fact I find it most amusing."

"What has happened here?" I asked; glad now, to be able to speak freely.

"I have been a fool, that is what has happened. I thought I had pre-empted the Count, but I was wrong. It was I who should have been here last night, protecting the girl, instead I have put her life in jeopardy."

"Was it definitely the Count then?" I asked.

"Yes, Watson. The imprint of the sole of his shoe is unmistakeable on the carpet, the very same imprint we observed on the sand near the harbour wall."

"Is Baddeley correct in his assumption that the windows were opened from the inside?"

"Yes, he got that much right." Holmes retorted.

"Do you think Elizabeth opened them for much needed air and the Count was waiting his chance?" I asked.

"I somehow doubt that my friend, I think he may have used some form of mesmerism, forcing her to open the windows against her will."

"She could be dead by now, Holmes; I just feel we could have done so much more for the poor girl," I said, sadly.

"I will reproach myself to the end of my days if that is the case, but I think we have time on our side."

"What makes you say that, Mr. Holmes?" asked Jacobs.

"In the account we read yesterday evening of these fiends, seven days was averred as being the time scale between the victim's first contact with the vampire, to their death. If I recall Watson's account correctly of your visit here yesterday, you were informed it was three days since Elizabeth had fallen ill, today then is the fourth day so, yes I do firmly believe we have time on our side."

"We have to consider though, that the poor girl had been ill before that time and it had simply not been noticed by anyone," I put forward.

"It is a consideration certainly, but I rather think the facts of the matter are as I have stated to you."

"Should we not be making plans then to find her?" I asked, growing impatient that we were standing around discussing the matter when she was in the clutches of this fiend.

"It would be no easy task I assure you." Turning to Jacobs, he asked, "What can you tell me about Haye Manor, Doctor, are there outbuildings for example?"

"Yes, many such buildings and stabling too, it is quite a large estate indeed, covering many acres," Jacobs replied, "there are rumours too of underground tunnels which connect it to the old manor house on Colway Lane."

"You see, if the Count is to be believed and gentlemen, I do believe him, then he has gone five hundred years without discovery during daylight hours. Obviously then, it would be a mammoth job indeed for us to find his whereabouts, particularly as the ground to search is so large. He has no doubt hidden himself ingeniously."

"What about the servant I encountered, could he not be apprehended and forced to lead us to Orlana and the girl?"

"An excellent question, Watson, but I fear such a plan would be doomed to failure. Either the man in question would not be entrusted with the location of the Count's resting place or assuming the Count to have the powers of mesmerism we so ascribe to him, then this particular servant would be so mesmerised he would be unable to tell us what we need to know."

"But the girl, Holmes!" I cried.

"Rest assured she is safe for now. The added danger of course is, if we were somehow to find Orlana and destroy him, it may be then that we may never find the girl."

"But Holmes, even though this vampire must sleep during the hours of daylight, this mortal helper of his does not, he may take it upon himself to harm the girl. I can vouch for myself that is he is a brute."

"No, Watson. He would surely be in mortal fear of the Count's retribution if he did so. No, she is safe."

"What then, are we to do?" Jacobs asked.

"I suggest, Doctor, that you repair to your surgery, Watson and I will endeavour to have a normal day as is possible under the circumstances. Will you please be so good as to join us at Mrs. Heidler's around six this evening, it needs to be early as we will hold a council of war, for it is war we surely have to wage and then I think we will all be in need of an early night for I have an early start in mind for us tomorrow morning."

This was agreed by Jacobs and he set off immediately for his surgery.

At the bottom of the stairs, we again encountered that most obnoxious inspector. "Ah Mr. Holmes, things have moved on somewhat whilst you have been upstairs. I am off now to arrest the miscreant, however there is one point I would like to clear up, it has no bearing on the matter now of course."

"What point is that, Inspector?" Holmes asked of him.

"Actually, it is the doctor here I need to address the question to."

"Very well, Inspector, please do so," I said curtly.

"I have a note here which you sent to Mrs. Hannington, a very queer thing it is too, could you explain the contents?"

I looked at Holmes entreatingly. "It is easily explained, Baddeley. Watson is extremely modest and would be loathe to tell you himself, but he is at the forefront of certain alternative remedies that are being tested at the moment," Holmes replied, his powers of invention to the fore.

"Yes," said I, joining in, "it is all to do with the power of positive thought, Inspector."

"Thank you, gentlemen," he said, looking rather exasperated.

"Who is this miscreant you are about to take into custody?" inquired Holmes.

"Once again, it is the simple solution that was staring you in the face that you failed to notice. The abductor, although I have every reason to suppose the girl was in on it too and a more than willing participant, is none other than the boy who delivered

Dr. Watson's note, one Nathaniel Heidler, a local boy," he said triumphantly.

"But that is preposterous," I cried.

"Not at all, Doctor. Mrs. Hannington has told me of his repeated visits here and his determined efforts to see young Elizabeth. She rebuffed him every time and he was now ready to take more desperate measures. He seized his chance when you handed him a note to deliver. I believe he inserted a coded message into the envelope, which Mrs. Hannington had discarded on the hall table."

"How ingenious of him, Inspector and then what happened?"

"Bawden must have dropped off to sleep at one point and Elizabeth crept downstairs, read the message, waited until Bawden had gone to bed, opened the French windows to signal or call to the boy and then left by the front door."

"How are we to explain her knowing there was a coded message there waiting for her, did the boy send a previous coded message, saying wait for my next coded message? No, no, Inspector, it will not do."

"There you are again, quibbling over the tiny details, my facts fit the case perfectly, Mr. Holmes," he crowed, "you will not admit you are beaten by good old police efficiency."

"If I ever chance to be beaten by good old police efficiency then I will be more than happy to admit to it, but, Inspector Baddeley, I will tell you this; every one of your facts is wrong in every detail, but there is *one* small point I would wish to clear up. I would be most intrigued to hear your account of how you rose to your present rank in your profession, for you are absolutely and totally devoid of reason."

Baddeley stormed off, red faced, I felt the uncontrollable urge to laugh and indeed, would have done so were it not for the face of a tearful Mrs. Hannington looking through the window at me.

"Before we go, Watson, I must have a word with the good lady here," said Holmes.

"Mrs. Hannington, it is my intention to return your niece to you safe and well tomorrow morning. If I am able to accomplish this I must ask you not to speak further about this matter to anyone, including the police."

"Do you know where she is then?" she asked tearfully.

"I have suppositions, but no proofs, all I can do is to ask you to trust me implicitly," Holmes implored.

"I have trusted you once already and now my niece is gone."

"I know it is not easy for you, but you must trust me one more time, Mrs. Hannington," Holmes implored again.

"But what about the Heidler boy? He must surely be at the bottom of this?" Mrs. Hannington asked, growing angry.

"He has nothing to do with this matter of your niece's disappearance, he is devoted to Elizabeth and you have wronged him. I believe him to be an exceptional young man." Holmes told her.

"Very well, if you can keep your promise to return Elizabeth to me, then I will not say any more about this to anyone, I can see you are not going to take me into your confidence so it must be a blind faith I have in you, but faith I have."

CHAPTER FIFTEEN

"Is there not anymore that we can do today to assist Miss Hill?" I asked. "It goes against the grain to be doing nothing while she is in mortal peril."

"Please be assured old chap, she is, as I have said, perfectly safe for now. But I fear I may have brought the wrath of Mrs. Heidler upon the both of us, notwithstanding your budding romance with the good lady."

"Really, Holmes, there is no romance, budding or otherwise," I protested.

"Watson, my observational skills are second to none, even though I say so myself and my deductions on this occasion are correct in spite of your protestations to the contrary."

"Well, as you say, Holmes," I admitted, "I do feel as though there may be a burgeoning romance. I am certainly enraptured by Beatrice, but I have to be sure in my own mind that she appreciates such attentions and that my regard for her is not borne out of the fact she resembles Mary so."

"There can be no doubt in my mind, my friend, that she welcomes your attentions, the other matter, alas, I cannot answer for you," Holmes said kindly.

"I have to confess that I have suffered pangs of guilt over my feelings for her. It is not that long ago when it was Mary that merited all my attention and love."

"I feel sure, my dear fellow, that Mrs. Watson would wish you to continue your life and love again, knowing that the love you had for her will never die. I think you have much to offer a wife, Watson."

"Perhaps so, Holmes, perhaps so, thank you for your kind words, but I cannot allow myself to think about the future while we have this grim business to attend to."

The forecast Holmes had ventured of the reception we would encounter when we returned to Mrs. Heidler's proved to be correct. Beatrice was standing in the parlour, arms folded, looking most formidable.

"Gentlemen, I must ask you to leave."

"Beatrice................." I started.

"No, John, do not say a word, this is already difficult enough for me. I have just come from the police house where they have Nathaniel on a false charge. I come from a proud family, never was there any hint of trouble with the police and Nathaniel has been brought up to be God-fearing and honest. Within a little over two days of your arrival here, he has been placed in danger by you Mr. Holmes, by his delivery of a note concocted between the two of you and now finds himself under arrest. I will not allow such things to happen."

"Mrs. Heidler, Dr. Watson has to be absolved of blame, the missive was a concoction of my own which the good doctor kindly put his name to in order that the note should be read and acted upon. It is I alone who have brought this calamity on you, but I believe I can yet rectify this situation."

"And because of that note," she continued, as if Holmes had not spoken, "Nathaniel is under lock and key. Do you not understand?" she said, weeping, "he is my life and I will not allow anything or anyone to come between us. Please, gentlemen, collect your belongings and leave immediately."

Had it not been for the opportune arrival of the young man in question, then we surely would have found ourselves in the street.

"No, Mother, they must not leave, they must stay I beg of you," he entreated.

"Nathaniel!" she cried and ran to him, embracing him, "are you really free, have they let you go for good?"

"Yes. I managed to persuade them that I had nothing to do with Elizabeth's abduction," Nathaniel explained, his mother clinging onto him for dear life.

"Mr. Holmes," said the boy, "you told me she would be safe."

"I truly thought she would be. I made a grave miscalculation, I am sorry, Nathaniel," Holmes said.

"Then, where is she? Who has her?"

"I believe I know where she is and God willing, I will restore her to her aunt and to you tomorrow."

"Tomorrow? tomorrow? Why can't you act now?"

"It seems to be the way of things at the moment, that I should be asking people to put their trust in me. I must ask you to do the same. If I impart any more knowledge of this affair to you, it will surely put your life in danger and I have caused your mother far too much hurt already. If you will excuse us, we will go and gather our belongings together."

"No, Mr. Holmes," Mrs. Heidler said firmly, "and John, you are both to stay. I don't profess to know what is going on here, but in some way I think both Nathaniel and Lyme need you at the moment."

"Mrs. Heidler, fanciful as it may sound, I believe Lyme does indeed need us," Holmes said.

I have no firm recollection of how Holmes and I spent the rest of the day until Jacobs called around the hour of six o' clock. No doubt we talked, we walked, we dined and there is no doubt, either, that during each of those actions I had the foreboding it would be our last talk, our last walk, our last meal together.

I always had the greatest confidence in Holmes's ability to defeat any adversary and time and time again I was proved right in even the tightest corners we had found ourselves in, but this inhuman fiend we were to face now was of a different ilk altogether and I had the gravest doubts that we could effect his destruction without it also meaning ours. When Jacobs knocked on the door at six o' clock, it sounded for all the world like a death knell.

Before we could begin, Beatrice came in to the parlour. "Mr. Holmes, a package came for you earlier, with all that was going on, it completely slipped my mind."

"Excellent, thank you Mrs. Heidler."

It was a very small package indeed and after unravelling it, he held up the singular content, a gleaming silver bullet. "Very pretty don't you think, Watson? Fashioned to my specifications so it will slide very easily into the chamber of your very handy revolver, handle with care my friend."

"Have you a plan of action, Mr. Holmes?" asked Jacobs who was no doubt eager to return to the bosom of his family.

"As you know, I have stated my belief that the girl is safe and will remain so for two days at least, however, I propose that we act tonight, or to be more exact, in the early hours of the coming morning," Holmes said.

"How do you intend that we proceed?" I inquired.

"I propose that we gain admittance to Haye Manor an hour or so before dawn, hopefully then, as the Count flees the coming light, we can follow him to his resting place and thence to the girl."

"Gaining admittance will not be as easy as you make it sound, Holmes, we will have the Count's servant to contend with and presumably Rose and Orlana himself, plus of course he will surely be expecting us."

"Yes, Watson there will be great and grave difficulties in so doing, but I fear there are no alternatives to this course of action."

Holmes let his words sink in, then continued, "We do have a weapon that is the most valuable of all."

"What is that, Holmes?" I asked.

"The Count's fear of us......it may yet prove to be his undoing."

"Or ours, Holmes," I added.

"Yes, my old friend......or ours."

Jacobs rose to his feet, "If there is nothing more, Mr. Holmes, I would like to return to my family. They are most precious to me and it is for them I am taking these actions you propose."

"Yes, of course you must go back, we will meet outside here an hour and a quarter before dawn for the short walk to Haye Manor."

"What would you have me say to Sarah, Mr. Holmes?"

"You must say as much or as little as you see fit, Doctor."

"Very well, goodnight to you both."

"Goodnight, Dr. Jacobs, please remember to wear dark clothing and to have a crucifix about your person."

What thoughts must have been going through my friend's mind as he went home to spend inestimable time with his family, Sarah and those two dear boys Arthur and Cecil?

"Do you not think, Holmes. "I ventured, "that Orlana, knowing we would almost certainly be searching the manor, might have moved on to pastures new?"

"I fear not, Watson. Indeed, I think it is precisely the reason that he expects such a search to take place, which leads me to believe he will be there to greet us in person."

"A confrontation is unavoidable then, Holmes?"

"Yes, my dear, dear friend it is. My talk earlier of following him to his resting place was rather less than the truth of what I fear will occur. Quite honestly, I have no clear plan in mind to deal with this devil, but I think the game is worth the candle, decidedly so."

"I would not disagree, Holmes, we are duty bound to try and rid the world of this monster, I only hope that if we come out victorious it will be with no cost to ourselves."

"As to that, even if we do come out victorious and, believe me, my old friend the odds are against it, it will almost certainly be at a cost of some sort to ourselves."

"And this evening?

"Spent in quiet contemplation although I have to remove myself to the beach at some point to collect a rather fine piece of driftwood I noticed earlier."

"Driftwood?"

"Yes, I rather fancy it can be fashioned into a stake fairly easily."

"The silver bullet may yet suffice for us."

"Yes, Watson, but we have not just the Count to destroy."

"Rose?"

"Yes, my friend, Rose."

"If you have no objections, Holmes, I think I will retire early. I am in no great hurry to see the morning come, but without sleep I will be of no use to you."

" Watson, you have always been of use to me and I hope it will always remain so," Holmes said warmly.

The bravado in those words did not go unnoticed by me. I smiled and bade Holmes a warm goodnight. I sought out Beatrice and told her some of that which had been discussed. I made promises to her I hoped I could keep and she, in turn, begged me not to venture out come the morning. As I climbed the stairs I had the memory of her warm embrace to guide me into sleep. When I awoke it would still be night, the chilling thought struck me; would I ever see the dawn again?

CHAPTER SIXTEEN

It is one of the mysteries of my life that in a time of crisis, when many folk would find it well nigh impossible to sleep, I have always been able to sleep like a log and the night before our confrontation with Count Orlana was no exception to this rule. It was only Holmes's repeated knocking on my door that bestirred me finally.

I dressed in the darkest clothes I had available to me and joined Holmes downstairs. To my surprise, Beatrice was there also.

"Good morning, John, I hope you managed to sleep well," she said a little tearfully.

"You must not worry about Watson on that score, Mrs.Heidler, he has the most profound ability to sleep through virtually anything!"

"I have made a pot of coffee for you, John and for you too, Mr. Holmes of course."

"Thank you, there was no need, I certainly did not intend for you to be disturbed this morning," I said.

"It was no trouble on my part I assure you; I felt I had to be here. I will go and fetch the coffee."

"Well, my boy, how are you feeling?" Holmes asked.

"Apprehensive, nervous if not downright scared."

"Fear can sharpen the mind so well though, don't you think?"

"And are you fearful, Holmes?"

"I am not by nature a fearful man, Watson, as you know, but I confess to feeling a mounting horror this morning. I cannot tell whether it is the horror of what we have to do or the horror of failing in our task."

Holmes was silent for a moment and then continued, "Watson, I know full well how the land lies between Mrs. Heidler and yourself. I will not blame you at all if you decide against coming on this mission with me, you have much to live for old fellow."

"As do you, and believe me I have no intention of letting you go to face this monster alone," I answered, "if you leave here without me, I will follow."

Holmes looked at me intently for a moment. "Watson, I cannot say with any certainty which way things will go for us this morning, but it might well be that this will be the last chance for us to talk together and I wish you to know that I am proud to have been associated with you these past fifteen years."

"But, Holmes, it is I who should rightly be the proud one," I exclaimed.

"Thank you, Watson and thank you for saying so my friend," he said, gently.

Beatrice returned just then with the most welcome coffee and we sat and sipped our drinks, both of us lost in our thoughts. Beatrice set down on the table two crucifixes, explaining, "I hope these will be of use, Mr. Holmes, John told me a little of your grim duty today and I would feel happier if you were both wearing one of these crosses each."

"Thank you, we will endeavour to return them to you shortly, Mrs. Heidler."

"I truly hope so Mr. Holmes, I truly hope so," turning away as she spoke.

Holmes looked at his watch, "I fear, Watson that our time is at hand, Jacobs should be here any moment now." He looked at Beatrice and me, his eyes softening, "I will wait outside. Watson, do not be too long, my friend."

Beatrice covered my hands with hers and implored me one last time not to go.

"I must go; it is my duty not only to Holmes, but to everyone who lives here in Lyme Regis. I will return, do not fear," I said in a confident manner which belied my own feelings somewhat.

"Henry, too, said he would return. He did not. Be careful, John, come back to me," she cried.

I wiped the tears from my own eyes, picked up my coat and joined Holmes in the street. We could see the figure of Jacobs, marching confidently down Sherborne Lane. The Three Musketeers indeed, I thought.

"Are we ready, gentlemen?"

"Yes, as ready as I will ever be I think, Holmes," I answered.

"Yes," said Jacobs, "I am ready too."

It was a still clear morning, the stars were in abundance and there was just the hint of a late Spring frost, our breath billowed out in front of us like ribbons of light and floated away. Our footsteps echoed loudly on the pathway, anyone lying awake in their beds hearing us go by, could not possibly have guessed where we were bound or what we would be doing when we got there. Gulls were calling and screeching in the skies above us. Somewhere close by, an owl hooted and swooped on a mouse or some such creature. Everything was just so resolutely normal and I was conscious of the fact that if we failed, this normality, this essence of life here, would be wiped away. The responsibility weighed heavy upon our shoulders. Once or twice on our journey I fancied that we were being followed, the merest hint of a shadow in the dark, but I put it down to my imagination.

Speech did not come to any of us until we reached the gates of Haye Manor.

Holmes said, "Gentlemen, from this point, we are truly in the dark in every conceivable sense. I suggest we try and stick together at all times, separated, we will surely fail and failure is not an option we can contemplate."

"I have my revolver at the ready, Holmes."

"Good, kindly pass it to me, my dear fellow. I fancy my aim to be better than yours my friend."

"Do you have any idea at all, Mr. Holmes, as to where we will find Orlana in the manor? "Jacobs asked.

"None, my dear Doctor, but I rather fancy he will find us as he promised."

We made our way across the grass, wet with dew, rather than the gravel driveway. Even though this cushioned our approach, it still seemed abnormally amplified to me. Once again, I had the curious sensation that we were being followed; Holmes put it down to my nerves. The archway which led us on to the heavy front door loomed large in front of us. Even had we contemplated such an action it was apparent to us there could be no turning back now.

We had formulated no contingency plan should we find the door locked. However, it opened wide with our first touch. The hall we entered into was dimly lit with candles sparsely placed and was wide and spacious. We inched forward step by step, half expecting something or somebody to come swooping out of the shadows towards us. The truth is of course, we had no idea where to search and if the Count decided against confronting us, then we would search in vain. The dawn would be here in less than an hour and our plans would come to nought. We explored the whole of the western wing in complete silence. I had the uncanny and unsettling feeling that wherever we went, unseen eyes were following us. The noises that old houses are prone to making, the creaks and groans of timber, made us all jumpy and I was much relieved when we found ourselves back in the hall some time later.

"The east wing then, gentlemen," whispered Holmes.

We had gone no more than ten yards down the corridor when the servant I had encountered before came rushing at us with an axe raised high above his head. He was swinging wildly yet with no real control. I was trying to ward off his swinging arms with my own, when Jacobs executed a perfect rugby tackle. He forced him down and grappled for the axe, "Go, go now...find the girl, I will take care of this fellow......go I tell you," he shouted as he struggled.

I hesitated, not wanting to leave my friend behind. "Come on, Watson, please my old friend, there is work for us too," Holmes urged.

The eastern wing of the manor appeared to be the mirror image of the western wing. Many rooms led off a central corridor, with a magnificent room at the end. In the case of the western wing we had encountered a splendid library. What lay in the eastern wing, we were about to find out. As we approached the double doors of this end room, we were conscious of a presence behind us. Turning, we came face to face with what had once been Rose Hannington, her white shroud, now torn, tattered and bloody. She snarled and hissed and then flew at us, her fangs bared and gleaming in the candle light.

"Quick, Watson, the crucifix!" Holmes cried.

I reached inside my pocket and pulled it out, pushing it into her unholy face. Immediately she backed away and positioned herself a few feet from me, snarling and growling like a wild animal.

"Watson, all my senses tell me that we are close to our prey. We need to get into this room and keep that vile thing out for we can have no chance against two of these vampires."

"If you open the door and slip inside, Holmes, I will hold her back somehow and try and join you," I said with confidence where there was none. "Go my friend."

As Holmes opened the door, the creature rushed forward again. I thrust out the crucifix once more and she retreated. It was a pretty problem I faced, I desperately wanted to join Holmes, but to leave the way forward for this undead thing to follow would spell certain doom for us. I glanced at the wall where several pictures were hanging, keeping my eye all the while on that monstrosity. I pulled one down off the wall and deftly as I could with one hand, I removed the chain on which the painting had been hanging. As quickly as was humanly possible, I forced the crucifix between one of the links of the chain and tied the two ends of the chain together in a knot. The creature, seeing my hand was no longer outstretched, rushed at me with unnatural speed. All my senses told me to run, but I waited until she was upon me, until the very moment I could feel her foul breath on my neck and at that precise moment threw the chain over her head. She emitted blood curdling screams and her hands scorched and blackened as she desperately tried to remove the crucifix from around her neck.

I took my chance and followed Holmes into the room. It seemed pitch black, but as my eyes became accustomed to what little light there was, I could see Holmes standing to my left and directly in front of me in what seemed to be some kind of recess, stood the Count. He was standing behind a huge desk and laid out on the surface of that desk was Elizabeth.

"Dr. Watson, I am so glad you could join us. I take it from the screams I heard, that you have done some foul mischief to my bride. Your punishment will reflect that deed, believe me." the Count greeted me with.

"It is I who seek your destruction, Count. Can you not allow the doctor to go; is one soul not enough for your evil appetite?" Holmes beseeched.

"Neither of you is going anywhere ever again, I promised you death, gentlemen if you continued to interfere with my plans, my warning has not been heeded and I am a man of my word."

"Sooner or later, Count, you will surely meet your end. That goal may not now be in our reach, but it will happen one day and your miserable existence will be finished," said my friend bravely.

"Have I not told you already, do you not yet grasp it, I am immortal," he roared venomously.

"You are putrid, rotting as the years go by, degenerating cell by cell," Holmes said calmly, "your very contact with humanity damns you."

I could see he was trying to goad the Count into some desperate action, some weakness perhaps that Holmes could exploit or to divert his attention so I could act, but I was both weapon less and powerless. Somewhere behind me I heard the soft, but unmistakeable sound of a door being opened, was there another of these creatures here with us? What chance had we now?

"I will not let you spout further, Mr. Holmes, I only wish I had the time to organise a slow death for you."

"I do not fear death, it is to become like you that I fear most, to live such a miserable afterlife. Death will be all the more sweeter knowing I will not become a wretched, pitiable figure such as yourself," Holmes said defiantly.

"If becoming like me is truly the thing you fear the most, then I may yet be able to accommodate you. How amusing it would be to turn you into the very thing you seek to destroy," the Count snarled.

He stepped out from behind the desk and rushed towards Holmes. Two things happened then, almost at once, Holmes reached into his pocket and brought out my revolver, before he could even get a shot off, the Count was upon him with inhuman speed and I heard the sound of tearing flesh. Holmes crumpled and lay quite, quite still on the floor. I knew in that instant that Holmes was dead. My friend was no more. We had failed and I had failed him that needed me most.

While Orlana was launching his merciless attack on Holmes, I sensed, rather than saw, a figure run past me to the desk, pick up Elizabeth, sling her over his shoulder and make off with her all in one fluid movement.

The Count now turned his attention to me. I was still standing there, transfixed; the thought of escape had not entered my head with my friend lying there dead. My only feeling was that of rage towards this creature that had ended my friend's existence.

"You were given fair warning, Doctor, your friend has died for nothing and now the same fate awaits you." With that he rushed wildly at me.

He grabbed me by the throat in a vice like grip and lifted me bodily clear off the floor. I was thrown over the now empty desk. I had no means of fighting back, the crucifix was gone and I knew my end was near, I prayed it would be quick and painless. Futile as it was as the Count's face hovered above mine, my arms thrashed wildly hoping my hands would alight on something that could be used as a weapon. I could feel the points of the creature's teeth upon my flesh, when my left hand brushed against something…velvet…velvet?…these were curtains…curtains!…

I could see a chink of light through them. Sunlight! As the Count prepared in that instant to end my life, I pulled on them with every fibre of my being, they began to give way and then, joyously, they plummeted.

The Count looked up in fear and alarm as the sun's rays began to fill the room. At that moment I sprang up and pushed, pulled and dragged Orlana onto the floor where the rays of the sun were shining directly.

I lay bodily across the fiend and my mind was filled with pity and anger for all the victims of this evil malevolent being, I thought of my friend who laid down his life to rid the world of this creature. I thought of Mary, sweet Mary. I thought of Beatrice. All the goodness of humanity seemed to flow through me, giving me a strength I had never possessed before, It was a rage, a righteous rage I felt. It coursed through my veins as the Count struggled to free himself. I was determined this thing would not live to see another day.

The Count's strength was ebbing away slowly, but still he was fighting hard to throw me off, bucking and twisting beneath me. I could feel his malodorous, fetid breath next to my skin and he shrieked and blasphemed in ways that I will never tell to another living soul. I was not aware of when the struggling desisted and then finally ceased altogether. I could not even tell you how long I lay there. I can only say that at some point I was aware of a bony, but firm hand on my shoulder.

"John......John, for pity's sake, please be alive."

I turned over, racked with pain from my efforts to hold that vile creature down, as I did so a grey film of large dust particles slid slowly, reluctantly from my body back onto the floor.

"Holmes," I whispered, "you are alive... But... I... you ...how?"

"Yes my friend, battered, bleeding, but by the grace of God alive, but where is the Count, Watson?"

"Gone." I heard my own words as though in a dream. "Gone, Holmes."

"We must not allow him to escape, we must track him down, time is of the essence."

"You misunderstand," said I, almost laughing with sheer relief, "he is gone, destroyed."

"You, Watson.........you did this thing?"

"Yes, Holmes," I said in a whisper.

He embraced me warmly and clasped me to him. "Not just I, Watson, but everyone who lives here is indebted to you, even though they may never come to know it. Oh, my dear fellow."

We walked away from the scene together. The particles of dust released when I pulled the curtains down, were settling on the floor and merging with the singular grey dust that now covered its surface.

Outside, much to our joy and relief we found Jacobs, also bruised and battered, but thankfully very much alive. "The Count's servant fled, I could not stop him, Mr. Holmes," he explained.

"I am confident the wages of sin will catch up with him, we will not worry ourselves about the fellow," Holmes declared, "besides, he will tell to no-one what has occurred here."

"I encountered Rose when I was trying to follow you. She was struggling to free herself from a crucifix that was coiled around her neck on a chain. She was screaming and cursing all the while, the most unearthly sounds I have ever heard in my life."

"You again, Watson?" asked Holmes, looking at me as a proud father would to his son. "Remarkable."

"I knew dawn must be fast approaching so I followed her to her resting place; she had by this time somehow managed to free herself of the crucifix and was resting quietly. I fashioned for myself a stake and drove it into her heart with all the force I could muster. I have never had to do anything as horrible as that and I hope I never have to do so again. For a moment I thought the creature alive again as she seemed to come at me, but the inhuman life that inhabited her body soon began to decay. I said a prayer for Rose as her body crumbled to dust."

"You did well, Doctor and you gave Rose back the eternal rest that was stolen from her," Holmes said.

"My God!" I cried, "what about Elizabeth, she was taken ...who has her...the fleeing servant?"

"I have her, Dr. Watson," said a voice behind us.

There stood Nathaniel supporting Elizabeth. "I overheard your discussion yesterday evening and was determined to follow you. I shadowed you all the way and when the Count's or whoever he was, attention was elsewhere, I grabbed Elizabeth and ran," he explained.

"You did well, Nathaniel," said Holmes. "I did wonder whether it was you who was following us so carefully."

"I did feel guilty leaving you with that Count, but I had to make sure that Elizabeth was saved."

"Yes, of course, Nathaniel, you did the right thing," I said.

"Dr. Jacobs," asked Holmes, "could you go with our young friends here to Silver Lodge? Mrs. Hannington will be expecting you, stress to her the part young Nathaniel played in the safe return of her niece, but tell her no more than that. I will call on her later."

I patched Holmes up as best I could and made him promise that he would accompany me to Jacob's surgery later, in order to have the wound on his neck closed up properly.

"I fear, Holmes, we have seriously disarranged Sir Peter's fine house," I said light heartedly.

"Perhaps, it will have the effect of ensuring that Sir Peter chooses his house guests with more care next time. Well, Watson, I am much in need of a hearty breakfast and I know just the lady to provide one." And with that he marched off towards Lyme.

CHAPTER SEVENTEEN

The sun was burning brightly in a sky once more unadorned by clouds, our steps were light, in fact we were almost running in spite of our weakened state. The joy, the absolute elation of being alive, when death had been so close to both of us, was a palpable thing, yet my exultation was tinged with a feeling of disgust and shame. As the Count's body crumbled away beneath me into nothingness, somewhere inside me, I too, as the instrument of his destruction, felt as unclean as he. I was aware in those life or death moments, I was being driven by a blood lust as strong as any this vampire had experienced. I resolved, if I could, to keep these feelings locked away inside of me, for they would do no good if voiced to anyone.

We arrived back at Mrs. Heidler's in no time at all. Beatrice leapt up as we entered. "John, John, you are safe, thank God," she cried as she embraced me. "Mr. Holmes, you are hurt, I will fetch some water."

She returned with a pan filled with cold water into which she plunged a towel, wringing the towel out, she mopped Holmes's wound with it, applying it with a great gentleness. "Have you defeated this evil, Mr. Holmes?" she asked.

"Yes, he is destroyed although all the thanks must go to my courageous friend here, he it was who finally sent him to oblivion," said Holmes.

Beatrice looked at me, beaming that most delightful and winning smile and then turned once more to Holmes. "Nathaniel is not in his bed, "she said pointedly, "I don't suppose.........."

"He is at Silver Lodge, Mrs. Heidler. I fully expect that on this occasion Mrs. Hannington will be more than pleased to receive him for he brings her a most welcome gift, her niece, Elizabeth."

"He was with you?" Beatrice asked, her voice raised, "in spite of what I had said to you."

"He followed us, Beatrice." I explained, "we had no idea of his presence until he rescued the girl from under the nose of the Count."

"It was a most brave and selfless act, Mrs. Heidler, he is a son to be proud of," said Holmes.

"He is his father's son, gentlemen," she declared.

The breakfast, when it came, was a mighty one indeed. Beatrice joined us at the table and between us we devoured every last crumb. No meal had ever tasted sweeter to me.

"What now, Holmes?" I inquired, between mouthfuls.

"My first port of call will be on Mrs. Hannington, I believe."

"After your visit to the surgery, of course," I said.

"Yes, yes, of course my old friend. I would not dream of disregarding the doctor's orders," he said, laughing.

I laughed too. "You usually manage to do so, Holmes."

"I will remind Mrs. Hannington of her promise to me, not to speak of our part in the safe return of her niece."

"And the police, Holmes?"

"Now that she is returned the search will be over. No doubt we can concoct a tale which will satisfy the authorities as to the circumstances of both her disappearance and her re-appearance. The body on the beach will be attributed to the mad dog as so described to us by the inspector, he can then return to his provincial duties and I to Baker Street."

"Not just yet though, Holmes surely. We still have a holiday to enjoy and you, your research to continue."

"I fear, Watson that holidays with you are far too much for even my iron constitution."

"But, Holmes......?" I started, only to be cut off by my friend.

"No, my dear fellow, you, of course must stay on and complete your holiday."

"I certainly have a wish to," I said, looking at Beatrice.

"Then so be it, Watson and now I must remove myself to Jacob's surgery if I am to have any peace today," he laughed.

The rest of that day passed off quietly, matters were arranged with Mrs. Hannington along the lines Holmes had mentioned. The police were informed of Elizabeth's safe return and the matter was closed, but not without a few rumblings from Inspector Baddeley. Elizabeth herself made such a dramatic, miraculous recovery that later in the day Nathaniel was able, I am pleased to say with her Aunt's full blessing, to bring Elizabeth down to Coombe Street in order to introduce her to his mother. She looked wonderfully well and I shuddered as I recalled that awful sight of her, lying across that desk, with the Count poised above her. How close we had all been to death at that point.

Later in the day I took a walk with Holmes at his request, down to the sea front. We strolled along, free of the cares that had so afflicted us during the last two days. We stepped up onto the Cobb and walked its length. Before we had reached the halfway point, Holmes grabbed my arm and turned me towards the town. "Look, Watson, behold Lyme Regis in all its glory and you, my dear fellow and you alone have preserved this place, have freed it from an evil which threatened to envelop and suffocate it."

"I was not alone, Holmes. Whatever we have achieved here, was achieved together, the three of us," I protested.

"The sad truth of it is, of course, that no one will ever know, nor should they be allowed to do so, the world is not yet prepared for such a tale. Let vampires remain as an old legend," Holmes said.

"I did have some thought to setting down an account of our adventure here, Holmes, if only to clarify things in my own mind and indeed, for my own *peace* of mind."

"Well, Watson, I can hardly dictate to you what you may or not write, but I really do feel that the public should not be made aware of what has occurred here."

"I agree, Holmes," I said, "the record I intend to set down will be purely for myself and no one else. I will write it and read it through. I may even then destroy it, although as it will be such a personal record, the thought of destroying it abhors me, so I have a notion to keep it intact and hide it where it will never be found."

"If you do so, Doctor, ensure it is well hidden, for even future residents of this fair town may be unduly affected by the events that have happened here, we have a responsibility not only to the present, my friend, but also to those times to come."

We walked together up Broad Street as Holmes explained he had to purchase one or two items. These proved to be two pipes, two magnifying lenses and two ear flapped caps. I did not need to be a detective to deduce their destination. Arthur and Cecil were thrilled with their new toys, but I pointed out a small snag in their game playing, in that they would both be Holmes and I would be left out in the cold. I was the storyteller, not the hero, they informed me. Humbly, I had to agree.

The evening meal was a complete delight. Beatrice, Nathaniel and Elizabeth were present and the girl displayed a most prodigious appetite. Of her ordeal, she remembered and knew nothing. Nathaniel had resolved never to speak of it to her. We discoursed long into the night, the young ones made their plans now they were free to do so and I wished them all the happiness in the world. My happiness was still tentative and it was too early for Beatrice and me to make any such plans. The feelings of disgust with myself I had experienced during the Count's death throes, still made their presence known and I needed to purge myself of those feelings before life could continue for me as I so wanted it to.

Eventually, drowsiness claimed us all. Nathaniel walked Elizabeth home, no longer wary of being out at night as he had been so recently.

I slept fitfully when for all the world I had expected to sleep so well. I tossed and turned and my dreams when they came were full of darkness and impenetrable gloom. I awoke with a start, convinced I could still feel the Count's icy fingers around my neck. I dressed hurriedly, not caring to be alone for a second longer than was necessary.

Holmes was already breakfasting when I came down. I ate very little, apologising to Beatrice for the waste of her fine efforts. After I had gulped down some coffee, I felt a little better. "Is it still your intention to leave today, Holmes?" I asked.

"Yes, Watson, my bags are packed and as soon as I have procured transport for myself, I will be gone."

I made my excuses and disappeared. I came back thirty minutes later with the very same dog-cart that had brought us here only days before.

"Holmes, with due thanks to Mr. Curtis, your carriage awaits you."

We drove the six miles to Axminster in lovely, warm sunshine much the same as when we arrived. The horse seemed to have its own ideas regarding tempo and we were fortunate to make it to the station on time.

Holmes turned to me as we were standing on the platform together. "Watson, I had to smile when those two lovely boys designated you, not as the hero, but merely the storyteller, for truly you are the bravest and most courageous man it has ever been my good fortune to know. I am, as I have said, proud to be your friend."

"Thank you, Holmes," I said. There must have been a cold wind blowing, for my eyes began to water, "and you are truly the best and wisest man I have ever known."

"How glad I am that you brought me to this place of ghosts and phantoms; I feel most invigorated," he said as he clambered aboard the newly arrived train.

"I think, Holmes, that Lyme is free of such things now."

"No, Watson," he said. "Lyme Regis will I suspect, always have its ghosts."

"I am of the opinion that our trip to Lyme Regis has been a life changing experience for us both."

Holmes nodded his agreement and had apparent difficulty in keeping his emotions under control. "Watson, it was our destiny to meet and become comrades and I firmly believe that time has not yet come to an end, but for now you may have a different destiny to follow. Farewell, Doctor."

"Goodbye, Holmes," I cried, once more feeling the effects of that keen wind in my eyes.

Holmes had been right when he opined that we would destroy the Count, but at some cost to ourselves. The cost to me was the mixed feelings I now experienced. I may have been the instrument of the Count's destruction, but I could not help feeling that a part of me died also. I could not express it in any other terms than that. Yet, I had a chance of further happiness ahead of me. I could not allow these feelings to blight that, somewhere there had to be the key to recharging my life.

I returned the cart to Curtis and instead of going straight to Coombe Street and to Beatrice, I elected, once again, to visit that fine church by the sea. I am not an overly religious man, nor given to praying, save only like so many others, in times of great crisis, but I knelt down in that quiet church and contemplated my life in solitude. I would hesitate to call it prayer. After a few minutes, spent thus, I wandered outside. Behind the church was a seat which afforded that magnificent panoramic view of the bay. I resolved to sit there to drink in that scene and to compose my thoughts before returning to Beatrice.

I could see a small figure sitting there already. It was the oasis of normality I had encountered two days ago; Lydia.

"Hullo again, Lydia," I greeted her with.

"Oh.....'morning," she replied, beaming at me.

"What are you doing then?" I asked.

"Just thinking," she said.

"Ah....I have just been doing some of that myself, Lydia."

"About what?" she asked.

"Well, life really I suppose," I answered.

"That's what I think about too when I am sitting here."

"Do you reach any conclusion?"

"Yes, the same as I always do," she replied.

"And what is that, Lydia?"

The answer, when it came was simple, direct and inherently true.

"Life is good." she said.

EPILOGUE

After reading through the manuscript many times, I went once more to the history books, also newspapers and periodicals of the time, searching for documentary evidence that these events had happened as Watson had chronicled.

My searches revealed very little. I did find a reference to a discovery of a body on the beach, in a faded newspaper which equated to the period when Holmes and Watson would allegedly have been here, but little detail other than that. Some of the surnames of the major players in Watson's story are still very much in evidence here, hence, no doubt the oral tradition of their visit, but again, subsequent enquiries found very little to either support or deny the story. I did have more luck when searching through an old Church register, for there I found a record of the marriage of a Nathaniel Heidler to an Elizabeth Hill in the Spring of 1901.Nothing more was to be found in the church records regarding the happy pair or their immediate family. Perhaps, when Nathaniel married, his mother then felt free to join Watson in London and become his wife. Mere speculation, I know, but it pleases me to think that it was so.

I managed to trace some present day Heidlers to Cornwall and although they were charmed by the story, they could shed no light on a Henry, Beatrice, Nathaniel or indeed an Elizabeth. I could not find a directory of Lyme for the period and therefore could not find a precise location for Mrs. Heidler's guest house, but I have every reason to believe it was the house I was residing in then, where the manuscript was discovered by that luckiest of chances.

Interestingly, one of the few cases recorded by Watson as taking place in 1896 is that of the 'Sussex Vampire'. What are we then to make of Holmes dismissing vampirism so scornfully in the opening pages? I believe, heretical as it may seem, that this conversation is a pure fiction of Watson's, no doubt added to the tale to give the readers the flat footed view of Holmes and Watson they had come to expect. My belief is that they knew only too well what vampirism was, due to their spine chilling encounter a few short months before in Lyme Regis.

CHRISTMAS WITH HOLMES

The Sussex countryside, the rolling downs, looked uncommonly beautiful even at this time, or maybe especially at this time of year. The heavy grey skies spoke urgently of winter snow to come. The very thought of snow elicited some magical memories within me. The Yuletides of my youth seemed to me now, to consist of endless days of snowball fights and sledging.

The world was different now. Innocence had been lost and would never return. A year had passed since the cessation of the Great War, that abomination that mankind had wrought upon itself. I had seen for myself firsthand the injuries and anguish inflicted on the flower of that generation. The world that I had inhabited with my friend and comrade, Mr. Sherlock Holmes seemed a long way off, lost in the mists of time.

It was indeed, at his request that I was making this journey. Holmes had invited me to spend this Christmas with him at his secluded house on the Sussex downs. Not that Holmes was ever one for fully entering into the spirit of the season, he tolerated Christmas as one might tolerate the visit of an especially garrulous aunt. It had been some little time since I had seen my old friend and I was looking forward immensely to spending some time with him.

I obtained a cab for myself on arriving at Eastbourne Station and settled back in it to enjoy the five mile drive to Holmes's humble abode at Fulworth. The threatened snow had now begun to fall, snowflakes danced merrily around the cab, creating swirling patterns in the air. I pulled my muffler closer around me and retreated into the furthest recesses of the upholstered seat. These old bones of mine no longer kept out the chill as once they did. As we pulled up outside the house I could see the tall, gaunt figure of my friend, framed in the doorway.

"Watson, my dear friend, compliments of the season to you," he cried.

"And to you too, Holmes, it is so good to see you," I answered.

"You have gained a little weight I fancy, Watson, nine pounds unless I am very much mistaken."

"I fear it is a trifle more, Holmes," I responded light heartedly.

"Come in my boy; let me see you in the light. Ah yes, the same old Watson, as blithe as ever."

"I only wish that were so. My body rebels against me on a daily basis. Some days I can scarcely move at all."

"At least, Watson you are still a man of words, if no longer the actions of yesteryear."

"If by that Holmes, you mean my writing, why, yes I am. Although I was acutely aware that my chronicles never really gained your fullest approval."

"Admittedly, I found your tendency to colour your narratives with a tinge of romanticism a little trying; sensationalism at the cost of science if you will, but latterly I have been putting pen to paper myself and the difficulties I have run into have only served to widen my appreciation of your own skills in this department."

"Thank you, Holmes," I said warmly, "I am glad that you have come around to my point of view at last."

We adjourned to Holmes's sitting-room, where much to my surprise at least some attempt had been made to acknowledge the existence of the festive season. A small tree stood in the corner, decorated in a small, yet tasteful way. Holmes's chemical apparatus stood in the opposite corner and this too had been gaily apparelled.

"A brandy and soda for you, Watson and then I have a surprise for you, my dear fellow."

I gulped down the brandy hungrily and remarked to Holmes on the suitably festive look his sitting-room had taken on.

"I felt a little touch was needed for the visit of my oldest and closest friend," he explained. "And I have other changes to reveal to you too. I believe in my last missive to you I explained that the fair Mrs. Hudson had sold up at 221b and had retired to a nursing home."

"Yes, you did and I have been meaning to pay a visit to our old friend and landlady."

By way of response, Holmes led me by the elbow into the passage and paused outside what I knew to be a spare room of sorts.

"I hope, Watson that my ability to surprise you has not entirely left me."

With that he opened the door and bade me enter. The sight before my eyes amazed and delighted me. Here was a re-creation of our old sitting-room in 221b. Everything was there in every detail. The Persian slipper filled with tobacco, the coal scuttle with its precious cargo of cigars, the correspondence affixed to the mantle by a jack-knife. The gasogene standing where it had always done so. Holmes's prized Stradivarius was lying casually in the basket chair and to cap it all there was a warming, roaring fire in the grate.

"Well?" queried Holmes, grinning like the cat that has got the cream.

"Bravo, Holmes, it's wonderful, it is our old room to a tee."

"When I heard Mrs. Hudson was selling up," he explained, "I took the opportunity to purchase, for a fair price, all the furniture you now see before you. The other embellishments were already in my possession."

"You have thought of everything, Holmes," I said, smiling as I noticed one of the walls of Holmes's house had now been adorned with a VR marked out in bullet holes.

"Yes and to complete the scene, I have you friend, Watson. Come and sit by the fire, it will be quite like old times."

I carefully removed Holmes's violin to a place of relative safety and settled myself down in the basket chair. It was hard to believe this was not our old sitting-room, so faithfully had it been re-created.

"Do you know, Holmes, at Christmas I very often find myself thinking back to the affair of the Blue Carbuncle and especially now, sitting here in my old chair by the fire. I am half expecting a hatless Mr. Henry Baker to walk into the room at any moment," I said, laughing.

"Ah yes," Holmes replied. "Mr. Henry Baker's goose which laid a bonny, blue egg. I too am visited by the ghosts of Christmas past, Watson, but it is the ghost of Christmas future I dwell on more and more my friend."

"How do you mean, Holmes?" I asked.

"You have known far happier Christmases than I, Watson, with your family, with your wives. I have always been a solitary creature save for you my friend and brother Mycroft and sometimes I feel keenly that in my single minded devotion to living by my wits, I might have sacrificed my life in other ways."

"But Holmes, you have lived an extraordinarily rich life, in which your name has become a household word. You were, in your way, a champion of the people, a champion of law and order."

"Yes, I do agree that I was able to put whatever modest skills I possessed to some good use, but at what personal cost to myself?"

"Has something in particular happened to make you feel this way? Have you had a visitor perhaps?"

"Good old Watson, you know me so well."

"It has been thirty eight years, my friend."

"Yes," chuckled Holmes, "I can still recall the look on your face when I greeted you with 'You have been in Afghanistan I perceive' and now here we are, old men with time having taken its toll on us."

"A visitor, Holmes?" I prompted.

"Yes, Watson, a visitor, none other than our old friend Lestrade, long since retired of course, to Bexhill on Sea incidentally. He is a very, very occasional visitor and just a few weeks ago paid a call with his great-grandchildren in tow."

"How is he?" I asked.

"He suffers, as we suffer. We sit and discuss old cases that we were all involved in, his remembrance of the part he played in them is somewhat sketchy, but rest assured my friend, I gently remind him of any mistakes or wrong turns he made," Holmes laughed.

"I am sure you do, Holmes. Good old Lestrade. He jumped to many an erroneous conclusion, but I enjoyed the fellow's company you know."

"As I did too, my friend. The occasion of his last visit, and who knows, maybe his last, was entirely joyful. Gone was the sallow-faced inspector of the old days, but in his place was a happy, doting great-grandfather, proud of his great-grandchildren, delighting in their company."

"And this got you to thinking, Holmes?"

"Yes, I began to think about the things I had missed out on, will now forever miss out on. Pondered how marriage and an acceptance of the softer emotions may have changed my life."

"It would have changed the lives of many others too, Holmes. Many criminals would have gone undiscovered and at liberty were it not for your intervention."

"I have no doubt you are right, forgive me, my friend for being so maudlin at this festive time."

Holmes poured me another brandy and soda and we warmed our old limbs by the fire. We reminisced and re-lived our past adventures and times as old friends do. What a life we had enjoyed together. A life, that despite Holmes's melancholia of this evening, was one neither of us regretted for an instant. As we talked on, the brandy coupled with the warmth from the fire took their toll on me and the arms of Morpheus claimed me.

"Happy Christmas, Watson." said Holmes, cheerily.

I looked up through bleary eyes. "What? Oh yes, Happy Christmas, Holmes. Do you know," I said, looking around me, "this could actually *be* 221b."

"Watson, where on earth have you been in that dreamland of yours? This *is* 221b."

"I.....I....I'm not at all sure. Tell me Holmes, what year is it?"

"Oh, Watson," he said softly. "It is 1895, it is *always* 1895."

CHRISTMAS AT BAKER STREET

I find it recorded in my notebook that it was during the approach to Christmas of 1902, that I had occasion to visit my friend and colleague, Mr. Sherlock Holmes. I had been busy with my practice of late and was now living in Queen Anne Street, whilst Holmes remained a permanent fixture in our old quarters in Baker Street.

I had seen little of Holmes recently due to both the new practice and new wife I had acquired and I knew from our last meeting in September of that year, that Holmes had been busy on some great affair of state. Discretion was his byword in such high matters and he had not confided in me precisely what knotty problem he had been called upon to solve.

I had bought Holmes a package of fine, mixed tobacco as a Christmas gift and with that tucked firmly under my arm, I climbed the seventeen steps to that familiar sitting-room, which had been the starting point of so many adventures. Holmes was stretched out in the armchair and greeted my presence with a barely perceptible nod of his head.

"Good morning, Holmes, compliments of the season to you."

"Thank you, my dear fellow, you are looking most bonny, my friend."

"Thank you, Holmes. Have you no case at present. I seem to remember that last time we met........"

"Ah yes, that particular problem has now been consigned to history, successfully, I might add," he replied. "It was quite a pretty problem too and one that for matters pertaining to national security will never be able to claim a place in the series of sketches you have from time to time inflicted upon the public."

"So you will be able to enjoy a rest over the festive period?" I asked.

"Yes, an enforced rest, but a rest all the same. The case came to an end two days ago and yesterday my presence was required for an audience with the Premier."

"High matters of state indeed then, Holmes."

"Yes, my old friend. In fact he very kindly offered me a knighthood for my services in this recent matter," Holmes said, matter of factly.

"How wonderful, Holmes! Congratulations."

"I refused his offer, Watson."

"But.......why?" I spluttered.

"At present, my door is open to all, Watson, from the most exalted in the land to the humblest. I make no distinction in the lives and positions of those who seek my help and I fear that the title I have been offered would put a barrier between myself and those in a less privileged position. I have the greatest fear that my skills would be frittered away on frivolous enquires from similarly titled folk. No, Watson, my mind is made up on the matter. I will remain plain, Mr. Sherlock Holmes."

"But what a perfect Christmas present it would be for a fervently patriotic subject such as yourself, Holmes."

"Your entreaties are falling on deaf ears, my friend and there is another reason too for my refusal of such an honour."

"What is that, Holmes?"

"The knighthood would have been conferred on me, not just for this recent case, but for the whole body of my work. I could not see my way clear to accepting any kind of honour if my friend and colleague were not to be similarly rewarded."

"Thank you, Holmes," I said, abashed and humbled. "But I feel I am not worthy to have any kind of reward bestowed upon me. I was merely your assistant."

"No, Watson, you were and are my friend and colleague and not in any way, merely an assistant. And as for the honour being a perfect Christmas present, well, I have mine here."

"What is that, Holmes?"

"You, my friend, you."

Holmes turned away as he very often did when the softer emotions infiltrated his normal self. He picked up his violin and began to play.

I recognised the melody instantly and as Holmes played the piece exquisitely, I found myself singing along.........

"Should auld acquaintance be forgot..............."

SHERLOCK HOLMES AND THE BUDGET PROBLEM

I would be guilty of an indiscretion if I were to just hint at the identities of several well-born and noble persons who have had reason to consult my friend, Mr. Sherlock Holmes. The very highest in the land it seems, have all found their way to our sitting-room. And the tale I narrate now indeed involves such a personage, he possessed a name renowned and revered throughout the land. At the time he came to consult Holmes, he held the position of Chancellor of the Exchequer in Her Majesty's Government, a post which illustrated well the respect he had earned from Her Majesty and her First Minister.

He settled himself down in the chair opposite Holmes and as he looked at my friend he appeared to be on the verge of tears, his noble countenance pale and drawn.

"Lord Darling, how may I help you?" asked Holmes in his gentlest manner.

Lord Darling looked across at me and seemed somewhat hesitant to speak. I stood up to excuse myself, but Holmes motioned me to take my seat again. "Whatever you have to say, Lord Darling may be said in front of my friend and colleague, Dr. Watson, he is the soul of discretion. To go further, I would say to you it is both or none. Now, how may we help you?"

"As you may know, I am due to give my account of Her Majesty's Government financial standing before the House tomorrow."

"Yes I am aware of that fact," Holmes remarked, now in his driest manner. "How does that concern Watson and me?"

"Whilst we are all only too painfully aware that we are in the grip of a recession, the picture is much blacker than even you can realise, Mr.Holmes."

"It has certainly resulted in frugal living even here in Baker Street; I have had recourse to refrain from ordering my finest tobacco and I now have to make the previous days dottles last for a further two days. Watson's practice has gone into liquidation and the bank is pressing for immediate payment."

"Holmes," I remonstrated, "did it occur to you that I may not want everyone to know that sad fact."

"Yes, my dear fellow, just before I said it. And now, Lord Darling, please tell me why you have to come to consult me on the eve of such an important day for you?"

"The plain truth, Mr. Holmes is that the government is in serious financial difficulties, we have given so much public money to support the ailing banking system that we are at a loose end and know not how to proceed, but that is only part of the problem."

Holmes was by now quite exasperated and lost no time in telling our distinguished visitor just that. "Lord Darling, I am quite exasperated, I do not see how I can help you with this particular problem."

"Bear with me," the statesman replied. "We had assumed that the banks had lost money through the mis-management of their directors and by awarding themselves huge bonuses, but when the books were examined by none other than your brother, Mycroft, we found this was not the case; the money had in fact been stolen fiendishly and cleverly. The audit was only completed yesterday evening and it was at your brother's insistence that I have come round to see you this morning and ask your help."

"I see, pray tell me, what sum of money is involved?"

"Mr. Holmes, it is in the region of £30,000,000,000," he answered with a grave look on his face.

Even Holmes looked taken aback at the mention of such a vast sum. I found it very hard to believe how this possibly could have happened.

"Do you have any ideas yourself who could be at the heart of this enormous crime?" Holmes asked. "I do have one or two ideas myself in that direction of course."

"All I can tell you, Mr. Holmes is that the name 'Lymelight' has cropped up once or twice, a pseudonym no doubt."

"I am glad to see that we are in agreement, hardly had you finished giving us the details of the crime when the name 'Lymelight' came into my head."

"Who is this 'Lymelight', Holmes?" I asked.

"A shadowy figure, Watson. Slippery as an eel, but with undeniable charm, a rogue with a twinkle in his eyes," Holmes replied. "He lives in relative obscurity on the coast, from where he makes his plans and spins his webs of intrigue."

"So you can help us, Mr. Holmes?" pleaded our crushed Chancellor.

"I'm afraid I cannot help you. The fact is I know how badly this government has run the country's finances and I think there are certain crimes which the law cannot touch and which therefore, to some extent, justify the kind of action that 'Lymelight' has taken. No, it's no use arguing. I have made my mind up. My sympathies are with the criminal rather than the government and I will not handle this case."

Lord Darling left, broken, by Holmes's refusal to handle his problem.

"Holmes, if this fellow 'Lymelight' has stolen such a colossal amount of money, what do you think he intends to do with it?"

A faint gleam came into Holmes's eyes, "Watson, my dear fellow, could you reach down the Bradshaw's and look up the times of trains to Lyme Regis?!"

★★

FOREVER 1895

Ghosts you say? Ghosts. Well, I am none too sure my experience is memorable enough to merit being called a ghost story, but all the same, here it is. You decide.

Long before meeting you chaps I managed to come into money, yes, through fair means as it happens, an amount that would keep me in luxury for a couple of years maybe. I left the Derbyshire hills behind and kicked out for London. No special reason other than I was young, it was there and I had money. I was able to acquire some decent lodgings for myself to go with my newly discovered lifestyle. I occupied the two top floors of a three storey house, which gave me a bathroom, a fairly large sitting-room and two bedrooms. I had no other plans than just to enjoy myself immoderately with my moderate and unexpected wealth.

The 1950's seem so drab compared with the 1930's. Endless rounds of parties fuelled my frivolous existence and for once in my life, I was popular. I was very aware that it was more than likely my money that made me so. The London of that time for me was not one of Museums, Art Galleries and history. I had no interest in Art or Literature. Life was there to be enjoyed. I did just that.

I very often found myself with overnight guests and on one of those occasions a young lady by the name of Tiggy was in the spare bedroom. This spare room led directly off the sitting-room. When she put in an appearance at luncheon, Tiggy was not a morning girl as you can see, she complained bitterly of the smell of strong tobacco in the room. I did not smoke and as far as I knew none of my recent guests had either. I assured her it must have been someone smoking a very disagreeable tobacco in the next door garden. Other guests who followed Tiggy also remarked on the odour and I too, came to smell it more and more.

Tiggy, being a spirited girl and in spite of encountering this unaccountable aroma more than once, always came back for more. On the occasion of her final visit, she was more spooked then ever. It seemed that in the early hours, the bedside lamp had been switched on and she heard a man's voice. The voice was not clear, but she thought that he was talking about body parts, for the only words she heard clearly were 'a foot'. Freaked, she was, completely. Never came back, poor girl. Wonder where she is now?

One morning I entered the sitting-room and was met with the stench of obnoxious chemical fumes. The landlady had prepared breakfast, but unless she had enriched it with various unsavoury chemicals, that was not the cause. That smell too, became an ever present.

I often heard footsteps on the stairs at all times of the day and night.Sometimes galloping, sometimes measured. As these began to be more apparent to my guests, I began to find myself more and more alone. The voices started not long afterwards, but these were audible only to my ears. I could never make out any words, but mostly it seemed to me to be the voices of two men. I began to curse the day I found this apartment. It felt like I was being driven out. I know what you are going to say, I'll say it for you, yes, driven out of my mind too.

Things more or less remained like that for a few weeks. I wouldn't say I learned to live with it, I still managed to be terrified although oddly enough I did not feel threatened, but whoever these men were, they were destroying the life I had made for myself. Somewhere at the back of my mind I must have realised that all this phenomenon had to be supernatural, there was no other explanation. The footsteps, unexplained smells and voices were present all the time in varying degrees of intensity. To this mix was added the strains of a violin which sounded mournful notes throughout the apartment. In the end, it beat me and I gave notice to quit.

As I closed the door for the very last time, the voices, previously muffled, now became suddenly clear. "Has he gone now?" and then the answer, "Yes he has, my dear fellow."

I stepped out into the street and fate had one last trick for me; the street was now wreathed in an impenetrable fog, through it I could hear the sound of horses' hooves and wheeled carriages clattering on the road. When I looked back, all was normal. I guess it was their house and they wanted it back.

So, maybe ghosts, maybe not, but I tell you what, chaps, if any of you are thinking of renting apartments, just don't, whatever you do, go to 221b Baker Street.

A LYME GHOST STORY

A new home, a new life. Something which had been on the cards for sometime, but now fully realised at last. A chance visit to an old friend in a quiet seaside town had given me the impetus to make the changes I needed to make and a few short months later, here I was. I had purchased a cottage in the old part of town with enough money left over to live fairly comfortably. It is a town much frequented by writers and artists and whilst I considered myself as neither one nor the other, I had ambitions in those directions.

I found myself a part time job to while away some of my time, the position was neither demanding nor exciting, just a little driving job. If nothing else, it gave me the opportunity to see more of the area than perhaps I would have done otherwise. I managed to get the cottage straight and almost homely within days, my possessions were few and my needs simple, as long as I had a home for my CDs and books, I was happy.

I noticed quickly how the narrowness of the street combined with the height of the buildings conspired to trap noise and amplify it. Conversations of a not particularly loud nature could be heard clearly at night when all else was still, but still I was surprised one night to be woken by the sound of a violin being played. I was only disturbed momentarily however, long enough to register the beauty of the playing before I fell back into a deep sleep. In the morning, I could not be sure whether I had dreamt the episode. I had never heard it being played before, but then maybe last night was especially quiet, then again it must have been around one in the morning and would I really expect to hear someone practising on their instrument at that time? It was hardly important anyway and I quickly put it out of my head.

A few nights later, I found my sleep disturbed again by the sound of the violin, I knew this time it definitely wasn't a dream. I sat upright in bed, listening and just as before, it was truly beautiful. I couldn't tell you what was being played, my knowledge of classical music was skimpy to the point of it being non-existent, but even I could appreciate the wonder of the piece, it was both hypnotic and oddly comforting. I glanced at my watch, one-thirty in the morning. I listened for a couple of minutes, then the playing stopped abruptly and although my night had been disturbed, I was strangely disappointed at the cessation of this music.

The next day was taken up with more mundane matters; work in the morning and in the afternoon I had arranged for a local electrician to have a look in the wiring in the cottage. It looked as though it had received no attention for a long time. He confirmed my fears after inspecting fully the intricacies of the electrics and announced it would need re-wiring completely and the sooner the better. It was an expense I had not budgeted for, yet I had to have the work done, safety was paramount.

That night, I was again awoken by the sound of the violin. This time my violinist, whoever he or she may be, was playing a more urgent piece; it filled my mind, my soul even. I was entranced. Strangely, it seemed much louder. I thought this must be due to the different nature of the piece being played. Yet, it seemed not only louder, but closer, too. I got out of bed, walked to the window and looked out into a quite empty street, all was peaceful out there and as far as I could tell, no one else was disturbed by this beautiful music.

The next day, I had the notion of asking around to see if I could shed any light on the violinist who felt the need to practice at such unsociable hours. In the end I thought better of it and one of the reasons was that I did not want it to stop. I had become enraptured by the music, dependent on it in a way, as though it was only for me and I did not want to take the chance that by asking questions I may inadvertently put him or her off from playing.

The following night, it was the same pattern as before. The music would wake me around one-thirty and shut off abruptly once more, a few minutes later. The difference this time, was that the music was undeniably louder and seemingly closer to me. If I hadn't known better I would have sworn that the music was coming from within the bedroom itself. I put my ear to the wall which connected me to the next cottage, it wasn't coming from there, but it was so very near. Again, I looked out of the window into the empty street. I don't know what I thought I was going to see, a man or woman playing the violin feverishly under the street lamp maybe?

The day passed in a dream, all I could think about was this strange, beautiful music which visited me night after night, invading my senses and that evening I was in a positive hurry to go to bed. I slept well, surprisingly, but was drawn out of my sleep once more by the sound of the violin. I can't really describe to you how this music made me feel, it was possibly the most beautiful melody I had ever heard or maybe, ever will. I looked towards the bedroom door for it seemed to be from there, where this spellbinding music was coming from. There was a dim light by the door which became a glow and gradually this nebulous shape became the figure of a man, his right hand gliding the bow across his violin. He backed away from the door towards the stairs, his eyes imploring me to follow. I was, by now, wholly trapped within this glorious, bewitching music and I followed, willingly. All the way down the stairs he went, playing all the time. Before I was hardly aware of the fact, I found myself out in the street. He was out there, still playing, although I had not seen him open the front door; in fact I knew he hadn't as I realised that I had turned the key in the lock. He looked at me one last time and this fabulous melody, this beautiful melody came to a sudden end. He was gone. I had no time to ponder on this, for there came a sharp crack from within the cottage and all at once the bedroom was engulfed in flames. There was a phone box on the corner and I sprinted those few yards in record time and dialled 999.

The first fire engine was there in minutes and I watched the crew go about their work. The flames were everywhere now, licking out from every window, the smoke billowing down the street, taking with it my dreams.

After a few hours, the fire was out and everything had been dampened down. The fire chief was sifting through the wreckage, no doubt looking for the cause of the fire. I was in a neighbour's house; she had very kindly taken me in and kept me supplied with an endless stream of coffee. All I could think about was how I would still have been in the bedroom had I not followed my violinist into the street. Was it a precognitive dream then? An apparition formed only in my mind by God knows what processes? I did not know, only that I had been saved.

There was a knock at the door and the fire chief came in, his eyes were full of pity for me. "Sorry sir, we weren't able to save much I'm afraid."

I mumbled something in return. "It looks as though the wiring might have been at fault. The fire started in the bedroom and spread very quickly through the rest of the house. Some of your books might have survived, but little else, save for this, which we found in the bedroom and somehow it wasn't damaged by the flames."

He handed me a violin. Unmarked, untouched.

★★★

TIMELESS IN LYME

Ever had the feeling you belong somewhere or maybe that somewhere belongs to you? It's how I feel about Lyme Regis. Something in the fabric of the place calls to me......fanciful? Maybe, but consider this:

I fell into a deep, peaceful sleep two evenings ago, of course it could have been induced by the cider intake of that afternoon, as could the dream I had. In my dream I was at the top of Sherborne Lane, a very ancient trackway, but it was a very different Lyme that I was seeing from there. Broad Street, the main street, was instantly recognisable although the shops were certainly different; they bore unfamiliar names and carried on businesses unknown to me. This, then, was a dream of the past.

The air was chilly and I wrapped my fleece jacket around me. I had no notion of the time, but I suspected it was early evening. There were a few people around, all of them dressed in what I took to be Victorian garb. There were one or two dog-carts outside the shops, but little activity. The whole dream was pretty much devoid of colour, almost monochrome in fact, except for myself. I could see I was wearing my red fleece, along with a pair of blue jeans. I attempted to interact with the passers by, but I was given a wide berth and wildly staring eyes followed my progress down Broad Street. I walked down to Cobb Gate and turned around the corner onto Marine Parade, standing silently watching the sea for a moment and the next thing I knew, I was on my settee, fully awake and musing over the particular vividness of the dream.

That was two nights ago, yesterday I had to spend some time researching the Victorian period in Lyme for the Sherlock Holmes novel I am writing. I was in the local library poring over old newspapers of the period when the following report caught my eye:

16 th January 1896

'There was a most singular occurrence in Broad Street two days ago. Several people going about their business reported that they believed they had seen a phantom. The apparition, if that's what it was, was attired in strange dress unlike anything the witnesses had ever seen before. They all agreed as one, that he was an oldish man and had a very peculiar air about him. He was observed walking down to Cobb Gate and after looking out to sea, promptly vanished, to the consternation of those present. No further reports have been received by these offices.'

14th January. Odd, that was the evening of my dream. Oh well, perhaps I had come across this report before and dreamt myself into it! Funny what the mind can do.

A new book was published here today: 'Lyme Past', really just a book of old photographs with historical references and footnotes, but very informative all the same. What really interested me were the lovely black and white photos of Victorian Lyme. I settled down on the settee to study them in greater depth. I used my magnifying glass to pick up the finer details of the shop fronts etc, all of which would help the accuracy of my proposed novel. There was one in particular that caught my eye, taken from the bottom of Broad Street looking up the hill. The street is not very busy, the blurb accompanying the photo says it was taken during the early part of the evening. I scanned the shops, buildings and people with my lens and noticed an out of place sort of figure walking down Broad Street. I looked more closely. I could just make out the grey hair and the glasses and although the jacket he was wearing is rendered dark by the black and white of the film, I, of course, knew it was red.

Told you I belonged.

****

DREAMS BY THE SEA

Dedicated to the memory of Duncan Ruffle 1979-2009

The sea is calm and expectant

On the horizon a flash of light

The sun casts its rays across the sea

Like the shadows of a unfurling hand

The golden light bathes the town

And people awake from their dreams

Dreams by the sea

The aches and pains of the day before

Are forgotten as the life enriching sun empowers them

The fishermen stretch and yawn

And gaze at the calm waters

They smile at each other knowingly

Today will be a good day for their dreams

Dreams from the sea

The sun reflects on the sails of the boats

The harbour is awash with light colour and noise

Pleasure boats and speedboats arrive

Their owners eager to sail

A flotilla twists and turns out of the harbour

Each man woman and child fulfilling their dreams

Dreams of the sea

The sea is calm once more

Fishermen have returned home with their catch

Evening takes its hold

A restfulness spreads over the town

Parents put their children to bed

And wish them pleasant dreams

Dreams of the sea.

★★

Acknowledgements

My thanks go to: Gill, my fiercest critic, who read and re-read and tried to keep me on the grammatical straight and narrow. If errors remain, they are mine and mine alone. To Duncan and Melody. To all family and friends for their suggestions and comments along the way. Thanks, too, to all the members at the Holmesian.net forum, for their encouragement and lunacy. Thank you also, to all the team at printondemand-worldwide.com, you made the whole process unbelievably simple for me. And thanks to Lydia, who, as always, gets the last word.

Links:

www.storiesfromlymelight.blogspot.com
www.holmesian.net
www.lymeregis.com
www.lymeregis.org